Abaft the Funnel by Rudyard Kipling

A Short Story Collection

Rudyard Kipling: A great Victorian, a great writer of Empire, a great man.

Rudyard Kipling was one of the most popular writers of prose and poetry in the late 19th and 20th Century and awarded the Noble Prize for Literature in 1907.

Born in Bombay on 30th December 1865, as was the custom in those days, he and his sister were sent back to England when he was 5. The ill-treatment and cruelty by the couple who they boarded with in Portsmouth, Kipling himself suggested, contributed to the onset of his literary life. This was further enhanced by his return to India at age 16 to work on a local paper, as not only did this result in him writing constantly but also made him explore issues of identity and national allegiance which pervade much of his work.

Whilst he is best remembered for his classic children's stories and his popular poem 'If...' he is also regarded as a major innovator in the art of the short story.

I0684164

Index of Contents

Preface

The measure of a man's popularity is not always—or indeed seldom—the measure of his intrinsic worth. So, when the earlier work of any writer is gathered together in more enduring form, catering to the enthusiasm of his readers in his maturer years, there is always a suspicion that the venture is purely a commercial one, with- out literary justification.

Fortunately these stories of Mr. Kipling's form their own best excuse for this, their first appearance together in book form. Not merely because in them may be traced the origin of that style and subject matter that later made their author famous; but because the stories are in themselves worth while— worth writing, worth reading. "The Likes o' Us" is as true to the type as any of the inunortal Mulvaney stories; the beginning of "New Brooms" is as succinctly fine as any prose Mr. Kipling ever wrote; for searching out and presenting such splendid pieces of fiction as "Sleipner, late Thurinda," and "A Little More Beef" to a public larger than their original one in India, no apology is necessary.

Erastasius of the Whanghoa

"The old cat's tumbled down the ventilator, sir, and he's swearing away under the furnace-door in the stoke-hole," said the second officer to the Captain of the Whanghoa, "Now what in thunder was Erastasius doing at the mouth of the ventilator? It's four feet from the ground and painted red at that. Any of the children been amusing themselves with him, d'you think? I wouldn't have Erastasius disturbed in his inside for all the gold in the treasury," said the Captain. "Tell some one to bring him up, and handle him delicately, for he's not a quiet beast."

In three minutes a bucket appeared on deck. It was covered with a wooden lid. "Think he have make die this time," said the Chinese sailor who carried the coffin, with a grin, "Catchee him topside coals—no open eye—no spit—no sclatchee my. Have got bucket, allee same, and make tight. See!"

He dived his bare arm mider the lid, but withdrew it with a yell, dropping the bucket at the same time. "Hya! Can do. Maskee dlop down—masky spilum coal. Have catchee my light there."

Blood was trickling from his elbow. He moved aft, while the bucket, mysteriously worked by hidden force, trundled to and fro across the decks, swearing aloud.

Emerged finally Erastasius, tom-cat and grandfather-in-chief of the Whanghoa—a gaunt brindled beast, lacking one ear, with every hair on his body armed and erect. He was patched with coal-dust, very stiff and sore all over, and very anxious to take the world into his confidence as to his wrongs. For this reason he did not run when he was clear of the bucket, but sitting on his hunkers regarded the Captain, as who would say: "You hold a master's certificate and call yourself a seaman, and yet you allow this sort of thing on your boat"

"Guess I must apologise, old man," said the Captain gravely. "Those ventilators are a little too broad in the beam for a passenger of your build. What made you walk down it? Not a rat, eh? You're too well fed to trouble of rats. Drink was it."

Erastasius turned his back on the Captain. He was a tailless Japanese cat, and the abruptness of his termination gave him a specially brusque appearance.

"Shouldn't wonder if the old man hasn't been stealing something and was getting away from the galley. He's the biggest reprobate that ever shipped—and that's saying something. No, he isn't my property exactly. I've got a notion that he owns the ship. Gathered that from the way he goes round after six bells to see the lights out. The chief engineer says he built the engines. Anyway, the old man sits in the engine-room and sort of keeps an eye on the boilers. He was on the ship before I joined her—that's seven years ago, when we were running up and down and around about the China Seas."

Erastasius, his back to the company, was busied in cleaning his disarranged fur. The ventilator incident had hurt his feelings sorely.

"He knows we are talking about him," continued the Captain. "He's a responsible kind o' critter. That's natural when you come to think that he has saved a quarter of a million dollars. At present his wants are few—guess he would like a netting over those ventilators first thing—but someday he'll begin to live up to his capital.'

"Saved a quarter of a million dollars! What securities did he invest 'em in?" said a man from Foochow.

Here, in this bottom. He saved the Whanghoa with a full cargo of tea, silk and opium, and thirteen thousand dollars in bar silver. Yes; that's about the extent of the old man's savings. I commanded. The old man was the rescuer, and I was more than grateful to him 'cause it was my darned folly that nearly bought us into trouble. I was new to these waters, new to the Chinaman and his facinating little ways, being a New England man by raising. Erstasius was raised by the Devil. That's who his sire was. Never ran across his dam. Ran across a forsaken sea, though, in the Whanghoa, a little to the north-east of this, with eight hundred steerage passengers, all Chinamen, for various and undenominated ports. Had the pleasure of sending eighteen of 'em into the water. Yes, that's so isn't it old man?"

Earstasius finished licking himself and mewed affirmatively.

"Yes, we carried four white officers—a Westerner, two Vermont men, and myself. There were ten Americans, a couple of Danes and a half-caste knocking around the ship, and the crew were Chinese, but most of 'em good Chinese. Only good Chinese I ever met. We had our steerage passengers 'tween decks. Most of 'em lay around and played dominoes or smoked opium. We had bad weather at the start, and the steerage were powerful sick. I judged they would have no insides to them when the weather lifted, so I didn't put any guards on them. Wanted all my men to work the ship. Engines rotten as Congress, and under sail half the time. Next time I carry Chinese steerage trash I'll hire a Gatling and mount it on the 'tween-decks hatch.

"We were fooling about between islands—about a hundred and fifty thousand islands all wrapped up in fog. When the fog laid the wind, the engines broke down. One of the passengers—we carried no ladies that journey—came to me one evening. 'I calculate there's a conspiracy 'tween-decks,' he said. 'Those pigtails are talking together. No good ever came of pigtails talking. I'm from 'Frisco. I authoritate on these matters.' 'Not on this ship,' I said: 'I've no use for duplicate authority.' 'You'll be homesick after nine this time to-morrow,' he said and quit. I guess he told the other passengers his notions.

"Erastasius shared my cabin in general. I didn't care to dispute with a cat that went heeled the way he did. That particular night when I came down he was not inclined for repose. When I shut the door he scrabbled till I let him out. When he was out he scrabbled to come back. When he was back, he jumped all round the shanty yowling. I stroked him, and the sparks irrigated his back as if 'twas the smoke-stack of a river steamer. 'I'll get you a wife, old man,' I said, 'next voyage. It is no good for you to be alone with me.' 'Whoopee, yoopee-yaw-aw-aw,' said Erastasius. 'Let me get out of this.' I looked him square between the eyes to fix the place where I'd come down with a boot-heel (he was getting monotonous), and as I looked I saw the animal was just possessed with deadly fear—human fear—crawling, shaking fear. It crept out of the green of his eyes and crept over me in billowing waves—each wave colder than the last. 'Unburden your mind, Erastasius,' I said. 'What's going to happen?' 'Wheepee-yeepee-ya-ya-ya-woop,' said Erastasius, backing to the door and scratching.

"I quit my cabin sweating big drops, and somehow my hand shut on my six-shooter. The grip of the handle soothes a man when he is afraid. I heard the whole ship 'tween-decks rustling under me like all the woods of Maine when the wind's up. The lamp over the 'tween-decks was out. The steerage watchman was lying on the ground, and the whole hive of Celestials were on the tramp—soft-footed hounds. A lantern came down the alleyway. Behind it was the passenger that had spoken to me, and all the rest of the crowd, except the half-caste.

"'Are you homesick any now?' said my passenger. The 'tween-decks woke up with a yell at the light, and some one fired up the hatch-way. Then we began our share of the fun—the ten passengers and I. Eleven six-shooters. That cleared the first rush of the pigtails, but we continued firing on principle, working our way down the steps. No one came down from the spar-deck to assist, though I heard considerable of a trampling. The pigtails below were growling like cats. I heard the look-out man shout, 'Junk on the port bow,' and the bell ring in the engine-room for full speed ahead. Then we struck something, and there was a yell inside and outside the ship that would have lifted your hair out. When the outside yell stopped, our pigtails were on their faces. 'Run down a junk,' said my passenger—'their junk.' He loosed three shots into the steerage on the strength of it. I went up on deck when things were quiet below. Some one had run our Dahlgren signal-gun forward and pointed it to the break of the fo'c'sle. There was the balance of a war junk—three spars and a head or two on the water, and the first mate keeping his watch in regular style.

"'What is your share?' he said. 'We've smashed up a junk that tried to foul us. Seems to have affected the feelings of your friends below. Guess they wanted to make connection.' 'It is made,' said I, 'on the Glassy Sea. Where's the watch?' 'In the fo'c'sle. The half-caste is sitting on the signal-gun smoking his cigar. The watch are speculatin' whether he'll stick the business-end of it in the touch-hole or continue smoking. I gather that gun is not empty.' 'Send 'em down below to wash decks. Tell the quartermaster to go through their boxes while they are away. They may have implements.'

"The watch went below to clean things up. There were eighteen stiff uns and fourteen with holes through their systems. Some died, some survived. I did not keep particular count. The balance I roped up, and it employed most of our spare rigging. When we touched port there was a picnic among the hangmen. Seems that Erastasius had been yowling down the cabins all night before he came to me, and kept the passengers alive. The man that spoke to me said the old man's eyes were awful to look at. He was dying to tell his fear, but couldn't. When the passengers came forward with the light, the half-caste quit for topside and got the quartermaster to load the signal-gun with handspikes and bring it forward in case the fo'c'sle wished to assist in the row. That was the best half-caste I ever met. But the fo'c'sle didn't assist. They were sick. So were the men below—horror-sick. That was the way the old man saved the Whanghoa.'

Her Little Responsibility

And No Man May Answer for the Soul of His Brother

It was two in the morning, and Epstin's Dive was almost empty, when a Thing staggered down the steps that led to that horrible place and fawned on me disgustingly for the price of a drink. "I'm dying of thirst," he said, but his tone was not that of a street loafer. There is a freemasonry, the freemasonry of the public schools, stronger than any that the Craft knows. The Thing drank whisky raw, which in itself is not calculated to slake thirst, and I waited at its side because I knew, by virtue of the one sentence above recorded, that it once belonged to my caste. Indeed, so small is the world when one begins to travel round it, that, for aught I knew, I might even have met the Thing in that menagerie of carefully-trained wild beasts, Decent Society. And the Thing drank more whisky ere the flood-gates of its speech were loosed and spoke of the wonderful story of its fall.

Never man, he said, had suffered more than he, or for slighter sin. Whereat I winked beerily into the bottom of my empty glass, having heard that tale before. I think the Thing had been long divided from all social and moral restraint—even longer from the wholesome influence of soap and water.

"What I feel most down here," said It, and by "down here" I presume he meant the Inferno of his own wretchedness, "is the difficulty about getting a bath. A man can always catch a free lunch at any of the bars in the city, if he has money enough to buy a drink with, and you can sleep out for six or eight months of the year without harm, but San Francisco doesn't run to free baths. It's not an amusing life any way you look at it. I'm more or less used to things, but it hurts me even now to meet a decent man who knows something of life in the old country. I was raised at Harrow—Harrow, if you please—and I'm not five-and-twenty yet, and I haven't got a penny, and I haven't got a friend, and there is nothing in creation that I can command except a drink, and I have to beg for that. Have you ever begged for a drink? It hurts at first, but you get used to it. My father's a parson. I don't think he knows I beg drink. He lives near Salisbury. Do you know Salisbury at all? And then there's my mother, too. But I have not heard from either of them for a couple of years. They think I'm in a real estate office in Washington Territory, coining money hand over fist. If ever you run across them—I suppose you will some day—there's the address. Tell them that you've seen me, and that I am well and fit. Understand?—well and fit. I guess I'll be dead by the time you see 'em. That's hard. Men oughtn't to die at five-and-twenty—of drink. Say, were you ever mashed on a girl? Not one of these you see, girls out here, but an English one—the sort of girl one meets at the Vicarage tennis-party, don't you know. A girl of our own set. I don't mean mashed exactly, but dead, clean gone, head over ears; and worse than that I was once, and I fancy I took the thing pretty much as I take liquor now. I didn't know when to stop. It didn't seem to me that there was any reason for stopping in affairs of that kind. I'm quite sure there's no reason for stopping half-way with liquor. Go the whole hog and die. It's all right, though—I'm not going to get drunk here. Five in the morning will suit me just as well, and I haven't the chance of talking to one of you fellows often. So you cut about in fine clothes, do you, and take your drinks at the best bars and put up at the Palace? All Englishmen do. Well, here's luck; you may be what I am one of these days. You'll find companions quite as well raised as yourself.

"But about this girl. Don't do what I did. I fell in love with her. She lived near us in Salisbury; that was when I had a clean shirt every day and hired horses to ride. One of the guineas I spent on that amusement would keep me for a week here. But about this girl. I don't think some men ought to be allowed to fall in love any more than they ought to be allowed to taste whisky. She said she cared for me. Used to say that about a thousand times a day, with a kiss in between. I think about those things now, and they make me nearly as drunk as the whisky does. Do you know anything about that love-making business? I stole a copy of Cleopatra off a bookstall in Kearney Street, and that priest-chap says a very true thing about it. You can't stop when it's once started, and when it's all over you can't give it up at the word of command. I forget the precise language. That girl cared for me. I'd give something if she could see me now. She doesn't like men without collars and odd boots and somebody else's hat; but anyhow she made me what I am, and some day she'll know it. I came out here two years ago to a real estate office; my father bought me some sort of a place in the firm. We were all Englishmen, but we were about a match for an average Yankee; but I forgot to tell you I was engaged to the girl before I came out. Never you make a woman swear oaths of eternal constancy. She'll break every one of them as soon as her mind changes, and call you unjust for making her swear them. I worked enough for five men in my first year. I got a little house and lot in Tacoma fit for any woman. I never drank, I hardly ever smoked, I sold real estate all day, and wrote letters at night. She wrote letters, too, about as full of affection as they make 'em. You can tell nothing from a woman's letter, though. If they want to hide any- thing, they just double the 'dears' and 'darlings,' and then giggle when the man fancies himself deceived.

"I don't suppose I was worse off than hundreds of others, but it seems to me that she might have had the grace to let me down easily. She went and got married. I don't suppose she knew exactly what she was doing, because I got the letters just the same six weeks after she was married! It was an odd copy of an English paper that showed me what had happened. It came in on the same day as one of her letters, telling me she would be true to the gates of death. Sounds like a novel, doesn't it? But it did not amuse me in the least. I wasn't constructed to pitch the letters into the fire and pick up with a Yankee girl. I wrote her a letter; I rather wish I could remember what was in that letter. Then I went to a bar in Tacoma and had some whisky, about a gallon, I suppose. If I had anything approaching to a word of honour about me, I would give it you that I did not know what happened until I was told that my partnership with the firm had been dissolved, and that the house and lot did not belong to me any more. I would have left the firm and sold the house, anyhow, but the crash sobered me for about three days. Then I started another jamboree. I might have got back after the first one, and been a prominent citizen, but the second bust settled matters. Then I began to slide on the down-grade straight off, and here I am now. I could write you a book about what I have come through, if I could remember it. The worst of it is I can see that she wasn't worth losing anything in life for, but I'e lost just everything, and I'm like the priest-chap in Cleopatra—I can't get over what I remember. If she had let me down easy, and given me warning, I should have been awfully cut up for a time, but I should have pulled through. She didn't do that, though. She lied to me all along, and married a curate, and I dare say she'll be a virtuous she-vicar later on; but the little affair broke me dead, and if I had more whisky in me I should be blubbering like a calf all round this Dive. That would have disgusted you, wouldn't it?"

"Yes," said I.

A Menagerie Aboard

It was pyjama time on the Madura in the Bay of Bengal, and the incense of the very early morning cigar went up to the stainless skies. Every one knows pyjama time—the long hour that follows the removal of the beds from the saloon skylight and the consumption of chota hazri. Most men know, too, that the choicest stories of many seas may be picked up then—from the long-winded histories of the Colonial sheep-master to the crisp anecdotes of the Californian; from tales of battle, murder and sudden death told by the Burmah-returned subaltern, to the bland drivel of the globe-trotter. The Captain, taste-fully attired in pale pink, sat up on the signal-gun and tossed the husk of a banana overboard.

"It looked in through my cabin-window," said he, "and scared me nearly into a fit." We had just been talking about a monkey who appeared to a man in an omnibus, and haunted him till he cut his own throat. The apparition, amid howls of incredulity, was said to have been the result of excessive tea-drinking. The Captain's apparition promised to be better.

"It was a menagerie—a whole turnout, lock, stock, and barrel, from the big bear to the little hippopotamus; and you can guess the size of it from the fact that they paid us a thousand pounds in freight only. We got them all accommodated somewhere forward among the deck passengers, and they whooped up terribly all along the ship for two or three days. Among other things, such as panthers and leopards, there were sixteen giraffes, and we moored 'em fore and aft as securely as might be; but you can't get a purchase on a giraffe somehow. He slopes back too much from the bows to the stem. We were running up the Red Sea, I think, and the menagerie fairly quiet. One night I went to my cabin not feeling well. About midnight I was waked by something breathing on my face. I was quite cahn and collected, for I had got it into my head that it was one of the panthers, or at least the bear; and I reached back to the rack behind me for a revolver. Then the head began to slide against my cabin—all across it—and I said to myself: 'It's the big python.' But I looked into its eyes—they were beautiful eyes—and saw it was one of the giraffes. Tell you, though, a giraffe has the eyes of a sorrowful nun, and this creature was just brimming over with liquid tenderness. The seven-foot neck rather spoilt the effect, but I'll always recollect those eyes."

"Say, did you kiss the critter?" demanded the orchid-hunter en route to Siam.

"No; I remembered that it was dam valuable, and I didn't want to lose freight on it. I was afraid it would break its neck drawing its head out of my window—I had a big deck cabin, of course—so I shoved it out softly like a hen, and the head slid out, with those Mary Magdalene eyes following me to the last. Then I heard the quartermaster calling on heaven and earth for his lost giraffe, and then the row began all up and down the decks. The giraffe had sense enough to duck its head to avoid the awnings—we were awned from bow to stem—but it clattered about like a sick cow, the quartermaster jumping after it, and it swinging its long neck like a flail. 'Catch it, and hold it!' said the quartermaster. 'Catch a typhoon,' said I. 'She's going overboard.' The spotted fool had heaved one foot over the stem railings and was trying to get the other to follow. It was so happy at getting its head into the open I thought it would have crowed—I don't know whether giraffes crow, but it heaved up its neck for all the world like a crowing cock. 'Come back to your stable,' yelled the quartermaster, grabbing hold of the brute's tail.

"I was nearly helpless with laughing, though I knew if the concern went over it would be no laughing matter for me. Well, by good luck she came round—the quartermaster was a strong man at a rope's end. First of all she slewed her neck round, and I could see those tender, loving eyes under the stars sort of saying: 'Cruel man! What are you doing to my tail?' Then the foot came on board, and she humped herself up under the awning, looking ready to cry with disappointment. The funniest thing was she didn't make any noise—a pig would ha' roused the ship in no time—only every time she dropped her foot on the deck it was like firing a revolver, the hoofs clicked so. We headed her towards the bows, back to her moorings—just like a policeman showing a short-sighted old woman over a crossing. The quartermaster sweated and panted and swore, but she never said anything—only whacked her old head despsiringly against the awning and the funnel case. Her feet woke up the whole ship, and by the time we had her fairly moored fore and aft the population in their night-gear were giving us advice. Then we took up a yard or two in all the moorings and turned in. No other animal got loose that voyage, though the old lady looked at me most repmachfully every time I came that way, and 'You've blasted my young and tender innocence' was the expression of her eyes. It was all the quartermaster's fault for hauling her tail. I wonder she didn't kick him open. Well, of course, that isn't much of a yarn, but I remember once, in the city of Venice, we had a Malayan tapir loose on Hm deck, and we had to lasso him. It was this way":

"Guzl thyar hai," said the steward, and I fled down the companion and missed the tale of be tapir.

A Smoke of Manila

The man from Manila held the floor. "Much care had made him very lean and pale and hollow-eyed." Added to which he smoked the cigars of his own country, and they were bad for the constitution. He foisted his Stinkadores Magnificosas and his Cuspidores Imperiallissimos upon all who would accept them, and wondered that the recipients of his bounty turned away and were sad. "There is nothing," said he, "like a Manila cigar." And the pink pyjamas and blue pyjamas and the spotted green pyjamas, all fluttering gracefully in the morning breeze, vowed that there was not and never would be.

"Do the Spaniards smoke these vile brands to any extent?" asked the Young Gentleman travelling for Pleasure as he inspected a fresh box of Oysters of the East. "Smoke 'em!" said the man from Manila; "they do nothing else day and night." "Ah!" said the Young Gentleman travelling for Pleasure, in the low voice of one who has received mortal injury, "that accounts for the administration of the country being what it is. After a man has tried a couple of these things he would be ready for any crime."

The man from Manila took no heed of the insult. "I knew a case once," said he, "when a cigar saved a man from the sin of burglary and landed him in quod for five years." "Was he trying to kill the man who gave him the cigar?" said the Young Gentleman travelling for Pleasure. "No, it was this way: My firm's godowns stand close to a creek. That is to say, the creek washes one face of them, and there are a few things in those godowns that might be useful to a man, such as piece-goods and cotton prints—perhaps five thousand dollars' worth. I happened to be walking through the place one day when, for a miracle, I was not smoking. That was two years ago." "Great Cæsar! then he has been smoking ever since!" murmured the Young Gentleman travelling for Pleasure.

"Was not smoking," continued the man from Manila. "I had no business in the godowns. They were a short cut to my house. When half-way through them I fancied I saw a little curl of smoke rising from behind one of the bales. We stack our bales on low saddles, much as ricks are stacked in England. My first notion was to yell. I object to fire in godowns on principle. It is expensive, whatever the insurance may do. Luckily I sniffed before I shouted, and I sniffed good tobacco smoke." "And this was in Manila, you say?" interrupted the Young Gentleman travelling for Pleasure.

"Yes, in the only place in the world where you get good tobacco. I knew we had no bales of the weed in stock, and I suspected that a man who got behind print bales to finish his cigar might be worth looking up. I walked between the bales till I reached the smoke. It was coming from the ground under one of the saddles. That's enough, I thought, and I went away to get a couple of the Guarda Civile—policemen, in fact. I knew if there was anything to be extracted from my friend the bobbies would do it. A Spanish policeman carries in the day-time nothing more than a six-shooter and machete, a dirk. At night he adorns himself with a repeating rifle, which he fires on the slightest provocation. Well, when the policemen arrived, they poked my friend out of his hiding-place with their dirks, hauled him out by the hair, and kicked him round the godown once or twice, just to let him know that he had been discovered. They then began to question him, and under gentle pressure—I thought he would be pulped into a jelly, but a Spanish policeman always knows when to leave off—he made a clean breast of the whole business. He was part of a gang, and was to lie in the godown all that night. At twelve o'clock a boat manned by his confederates was to drop down the creek and halt under the godown windows, while he was to hand out our bales. That was their little plan. He had lain there about three hours, and then he began to smoke. I don't think he noticed what he was doing: smoking is just like breathing to a Spaniard. He could not understand how he had betrayed himself and wanted to know whether he had left a leg sticking out under the saddles. Then the Guarda Civile lambasted him all over again for trifling with the majesty of the law, and removed him after full confession.

"I put one of my own men under a saddle with instructions to hand out print bales to anybody who might ask for them in the course of the night. Meantime the police made their own arrangements, which were very comprehensive.

"At midnight a lumbering old barge, big enough to hold about a hundred bales, came down the creek and pulled up under the godown windows, exactly as if she had been one of my own barges. The eight ruffians in her whistled all the national airs of Manila as a signal to the confederate, then cooling his heels in the lock-up. But my man was ready. He opened the window and held quite a long confab with these second-hand pirates. They were all half-breeds and Roman Catholics, and the way they called upon all the blessed saints to assist them in their work was edifying. My man began tilting out the bales quite as quickly as the confederate would have done. Only he stopped to giggle now and again, and they spat and swore at him like cats. That made him worse, and at last he dropped yelling with laughter over the half door of the godown goods window. Then one boat came up stream and another down stream, and caught the barge stem and stem. Four Guarda Civiles were in each boat; consequently, eight repeating rifles were pointed at the barge, which was very nicely loaded with our bales. The pirates called on the saints more fluently than ever, threw up their hands, and threw themselves on their stomachs. That was the safest attitude, and it gave them the chance of cursing their luck, the barge, the godown, the Guarda Civile, and every saint in the calendar. They cursed the saints most, for the Guarda Civile thumped 'em when their remarks became too personal. We made them put all the bales back again. Then they were handed over to justice and got five years apiece. If they had any dollars they would get out the next day. If they hadn't, they would serve their full time and no ticket-of-leave allowed. That's the whole story."

"And the only case on record," said the Young Gentleman travelling for Pleasure, "where a Manila cigar was of any use to any one." The man from Manila lit a fresh Cuspidore and went down to his bath.

The Red Lamp

"A strong situation—very strong, sir—quite the strongest one in the play, in fact."

"What play?" said a voice from the bottom of the long chair under the bulwarks.

"The Red Lamp.'

"Oh!"

Conversation ceased, and there was an industrious sucking of cheroots for the space of half an hour before the company adjourned to the card-room. It was decidedly a night for sleeping on deck—warm as the Red Sea and more moist than Bengal. Unfortunately, every square foot of the deck seemed to be occupied by earlier comers, and in despair I removed myself to the extreme fo'c'sle, where the anchor-chains churn rust-dyed water from the hawseholes and the lascars walk about with slushpots.

The throb of the engines reached this part of the world as a muffled breathing which might be easily mistaken for the snoring of the ship's cow. Occasionally one of the fowls in the coops waked and cheeped dismally as she thought of to-morrow's entrées in the saloon, but otherwise all was very, very still, for the hour was two in the morning, when the crew of a ship are not disposed to be lively. None came to bear me company save the bo'sun's pet kittens, and they were impolite. From where I lay I could look over the whole length of awning, ghostly white in the dark, and by their constant fluttering judged that the ship was pitching considerably. The fo'c'sle swung up and down like an uneasy hydraulic lift, and a few showers of spray found their passage through the hawseholes from time to time.

Have you ever felt that maddening sense of incompetence which follows on watching the work of another man's office? The civilian is at home among his despatch-boxes and files of pending cases. "How in the world does he do it?" asks the military man. The budding officer can arrange for the movements of two hundred men across country. "Incomprehensible!" says the civilian. And so it is with all alien employs from our own. So it was with me. I knew that I was lying among all the materials out of which Clark Russell builds his books of the sea—the rush through the night, the gouts of foam, the singing of the wind in the rigging overhead, and the black mystery of the water—but for the life of me I could make nothing of them all.

"A topsail royal flying free
A bit of canvas was to me.
And it was nothing more."

"Oh, that a man should have but one poor little life and one incomplete set of experiences to crowd into it!" I sighed as the bells of the ship lulled me to sleep and the lookout man crooned a dreary song.

welting into him with anything that came handy—sticks and besoms, and such. Lot endured that, being a tough man. Every time Lot was fired out he would wait till the old man was pretty well pumped out. Then he used to turn round and say, 'When's the wedding to be?' Dougherty used to ramp round Lot while the girl hid herself till the breeze abated. He had a peculiar aversion to domiciliary visits from Lot, had Dougherty. I've my own theory on the subject. I'll explain it later on. At last Dougherty got tired of Lot and his peacefulness. The girl stuck to him for all she was worth. Lot never budged. 'If you want to marry her,' said the old man, 'just drop your long-suffering for half an hour. Stand up to me. Lot, and we'll run this thing through with our hands.' 'If I must, I must,' said Lot, and with that they began the argument up and down the parlour floor. Lot he was fighting for his wife. He set considerable value on the girl. The old man he was fighting for the fun of the affair. Lot whipped. He handled the old man tenderly out of regard for his connections. All the same he fixed him up pretty thoroughly. When he crawled off the old man he had received his permission to marry the girl. Old man Dougherty ran round 'Frisco advertising Lot for the tallest fighter in the town. Lot was a respectable sort of man and considerable absorbed in preparing for his wedding. It didn't please him any to receive invitations from the boss fighting men of Trisco—professional invitations, you must understand. I guess he cussed the father-in-law to be.

"When he was married, he concluded to locate in 'Frisco, and started business there. A married man don't keep his muscle up any. Old man Dougherty he must have counted on that. By the time Lot's first child was born he came around suffering for a fight. He painted Lot's house crimson. Lot endured that. He got a hold of the baby and began yanking it around by the legs to see if it could squeal worth listening to. Lot stretched him. Old man howled with delight. Lot couldn't well hand his father-in-law over to the police, so they had it, knuckle and tooth, all round the front floor, and the old man he quit by the window, considerably mashed up. Lot was fair spent, not having kept up his muscle. My notion is that old man Dougherty being a boss fighter couldn't get his fighting regularly till Lot married into the family. Then he reckoned on a running discussion to warm up his bones. Lot was too fond of his wife to disoblige him. Any man in his senses would have brought the old man before the courts, or clubbed him, or laid him out stiff. But Lot was always tender-hearted.

"Soon as old man Dougherty got his senses together off the pavement, he argued that Lot was considerable less of a fighter than he had been. That pleased the old man. He was plastered and caulked up by the doctors, and as soon as he could move he interviewed Lot and made remarks. Lot didn't much care what he said, but when he came to casting reflections on the parentage of the baby. Lot shut the office door and played round for half an hour till the walls glittered like the evening sun. Old man Dougherty crawled out, but he crowed as he crawled. 'Praise the blessed saints,' he said, 'I kin get my fighting along o' my meals. Lot, ye have prolonged my life a century.'

"Guess Lot would like to see him dead now. He is an old man, but most amazing tough. He has been fighting Lot for a matter of three years. If Lot made a lucky bit of trade, the old man would come along and fight him for luck. If Lot lost a little, the old man would fight him to teach him safe speculation. It took all Lot's time to keep even with him. No man in business can 'tend his business and fight in streaks. Lot's trade fell off every time he laid himself out to stretch the old man. Worst of it was that when Lot was made a Deacon of his church, the old man fought him most terrible for the honour of the Roman Catholic Church. Lot whipped, of course. He always whipped. Old man Dougherty went round among the other Deacons and lauded Lot for a boss pugilist, not meaning to hurt Lot's prospects. Lot had to explain the situation to the church in general. They accepted it.

"Old man Dougherty he fought on. Age had no effect on him. Lot always whipped, but nothing would satisfy the old man. Lot shook all his teeth out till his gums were as bare as a sand-bar. Old man Dougherty came along lisping his invitation to the dance. They fought.

"When Lot shifted to San Luis Obispo, old man Dougherty he came along too—craving for his fight. It was cocktails and plug to him. It grew on him. Lot handled him too gently because of the wife. The old man could come to the scratch once a month, and always at the most inconvenient time. They fought.

"Last I heard of Lot he was sinking into the tomb. 'It's not the fighting,' he said to me. 'It's the darned monotony of the circus. He knows I can whip him, but he won't rest satisfied. 'Lay him out, Lot,' said I; 'fracture his cranium or gouge him. This show is foolish all round.' 'I can't lay him out,' said Lot. 'He's my father-in-law. But don't it strike you I've a deal to be thankful for? If he had been a Jew he'd have fought on Sundays when I was doing Deacon. I've been too gentle with him; the old man knows my spot place, but I've a deal to be thankful for.'

"Strikes me that thankfulness of Lot's sort is nothing more nor less than cussed affectation. Say!"

I said nothing.

A Little More Beef

"A little more beef, please!' said the fat man with the grey whiskers and the spattered waistcoat. "You can't eat too much o' good beef—not even when the prices are going up hoof over hock." And he settled himself down to load in a fresh cargo.

Now, this is how the fat man had come by his meal. One thousand miles away, a red Texan steer was preparing to go to bed for the night in the company of his fellows—myriads of his fellows. From dawn till late dusk he had loafed across the leagues of grass and grunted savagely as each mouthful proved to his mind that grass was not what he had known it in his youth. But the steer was wrong. That summer had brought great drought to Montana and Northern Dakota. The cattle feed was withering day by day, and the more prudent stock owners had written to the East for manufactured provender. Only the little cactus that grows with the grasses appeared to enjoy itself. The cattle certainly did not; and the cowboys from the very beginning of spring had used language considered profane even for the cowboy. What their ponies said has never been recorded. The ponies had the worst time of all, and at each nightly camp whispered to each other their longings for the winter, when they would be turned out on the freezing ranges—galled from wither to croup, but riderless—thank Heaven, riderless. On these various miseries the sun looked down impartial. His business was to cake the ground and ruin the grasses.

The cattle—the acres of huddled cattle—were restless. In the first place, they were forced to scatter for graze; and in the second, the heat told on their tempers and made them prod each other with their long horns. In the heart of the herd you would have thought men were fighting with single-sticks. On the outskirts, posted at quarter-mile intervals, sat the cowboys on their ponies, the brims of their hats tilted over their sun-skinned noses, their feet out of the big brown-leather hooded stirrups, and their hands gripping the horn of the heavy saddle to keep themselves from falling on to the ground—asleep. A cowboy can sleep at full gallop; on the other hand, he can keep awake also at full gallop for eight and forty hours and wear down six unamiable bronchos in the process.

Lafe Parmalee; Shwink, the German who could not ride but had a blind affection for cattle from the branding-yard to the butcher's block; Michigan, so called because he said he came from California but spoke not the Californian tongue; Jim from San Diego, to distinguish him from other Jims, and The Corpse, were the outposts of the herd. The Corpse had won his name from a statement, made in the fulness of much McBrayer whisky, that he had once been a graduate of Corpus Christi. He spoke truth, but to the wrong audience. The inhabitants of the Elite Saloon, after several attempts to get the hang of the name, dubbed the speaker The Corpse, and as long as he cinched a broncho or jingled a spur within four hundred miles of Livingston—yea, far in the south, even to the unexplored borders of the sheep-eater Indians—he was known by that unlovely name. How he had passed from college to cattle no man knew, and, according to the etiquette of the West, no man asked. He was not by any means a tenderfoot—had no unmanly weakness for washing, did not in the least object to appearing at the wild and wonderful reunions held nightly in "Miss Minnie's parlour," whose flaring advertisement did not in the least disturb the proprieties of Wachoma Junction, and, in common with his associates, was, when drunk, ready to shoot at anything or anybody. He was not proud. He had condescended to take in hand and educate a young and promising Chicago drummer, who by evil fate had wandered into that wilderness, where all his cunning was of no account; and from that youth's quivering hand— outstretched by command—had shot away the top of a wineglass. The Corpse was recognised in the freemasonry of the craft as "one of the C.M.R.'s boys, and tough at that."

The C.M.R. controlled much cattle, and their slaughter-houses in Chicago bubbled the blood of beeves all day long. Their salt-beef fed the sailor on the sea, and their iced, best firsts, the housekeeper in the London suburbs. Not even the firm knew how many cowboys they employed, but all the firm knew that on the fourteenth day of July their stockyards at Wachoma Junction were to be filled with two thousand head of cattle, ready for immediate shipment to Chicago while prices yet ruled high, and before the grass had withered utterly. Lafe, Michigan, Jim, The Corpse and the others knew this too, and were heartily glad of it, because they would be paid up in Chicago for their half-year's work, and would then do their best towards painting that town in purest vermilion. They would get drunk; they would gamble, and would otherwise enjoy themselves till they were broke; and then they would hire out again.

The sun dropped behind the rolling hills; and the cattle halted for the night, cheered and cooled by a little wandering breeze. The red steer's mother had been caught in a hailstorm five years ago. Till she went the way of all cow-flesh she missed no opportunity of telling her son to beware of the hot day and the cold wind that does not know its own mind. "When it blows five ways at once," said she, "and makes your horns feel creepy, get away, my son. Follow the time-honoured instinct of our tribe, and run. I ran"—she looked ruefully at the scars on her side—"but that was in a barbwire country, and it hurt me. None the less, run." The red steer chewed his cud, and the little wind out of the darkness played round his horns—all five ways at once. The cowboys lifted up their voices in unmelodious song, that the cattle might know where they were, and began slowly walking round the recumbent herd. "Do anybody's horns feel creepy?" queried the red steer of his neighbours. "My mother told me"—and he repeated the tale, to the edification of the yearlings and the three-year olds breathing heavily at his side.

The song of the cowboys rose higher. The cattle bowed their heads. Their men were at hand. They were safe. Something had happened to the quiet stars. They were dying out one by one. and the wind was freshening. "Bless my hoofs!" muttered a yearling, "my horns are beginning to feel creepy." Softly the red steer lifted himself from the ground. "Come away," quoth he to the yearling. "Come away to the outskirts, and we'll move. My mother said . . . " The innocent fool followed, and a white heifer saw them move. Being a woman she naturally bellowed "Timber wolves!" and ran forward blindly into a dun steer dreaming over clover. Followed the thunder of cattle rising to their feet, and the triple crack of a whip. The little wind had dropped for a moment, only to fall on the herd with a shriek and a few stinging drops of hail, that stung as keenly as the whips. The herd broke into a trot, a canter, and then a mad gallop. Black fear was behind them, black night in front. They headed into the night, bellowing with terror; and at their side rode the men with the whips. The ponies grunted as they felt the raking spurs. They knew that, an all-night gallop lay before them, and woe betide the luckless cayuse that stumbled in that ride. Then fell the hail—blinding and choking and flogging in one and the same stroke. The herd opened like a fan. The red steer headed a contingent he knew not whither. A man with a whip rode at his right flank. Behind him the lightning showed a field of glimmering horns, and of muzzles flecked with foam; a field of red terror-strained eyes and shaggy frontlets. The man looked back also, and his terror was greater than that of the beasts. The herd had surrounded him in the darkness. His salvation lay in the legs of Whisky Peat—and Whisky Peat knew it—knew it until an unseen gopher hole received his near forefoot as he strained every nerve—in the heart of the flying herd, with the red steer at his flanks. Then, being only an over-worked cayuse. Whisky Peat fell, and the red steer fancied that there was something soft on the ground.

It was Michigan, Jim and Lafe who at last brought the herd to a standstill as the dawn was breaking. "What's come to The Corpse?" quoth Lafe. Jim loosened the girths of his quivering pony and made answer slowly: "Onless I'm a blamed fool, the gentleman is now livin' up to his durned appellation 'bout fifteen miles back—what there is of him and the cayuse." "Let's go and look," said Lafe, shuddering slightly, for the morning air, you must understand, was raw. "Let's go to—a much hotter place than Texas," responded Jim. "Get the steers to the Junction first. Guess what's left of The Corpse will keep."

And it did. And that was how the fat man in Chicago got his beef. It belonged to the red steer.

The History of a Fall

MereEnglish will not do justice to the event. Let us attempt it according to the custom of the French. Thus and so following:

Listen to a history of the most painful—and of the most true. You others, the Grovernors, the Lieutenant-Governors, and the Commissionaires of the Oriental Indias.

It is you, foolishly outside of the truth in prey to illusions so blind that I of them remain so stupefied—it is to you that I address myself!

Know you Sir Cyril Wollobie, K.C.S.I., C.M.G., and all the other little things?

He was of the Sacred Order of Yourself—a man responsible enormously—charged of the conservation of millions . . .

Of people. That is understood. The Indian Government conserves not its rupees.

He was the well-loved of kings. I have seen the Viceroy—which is the Lorr-Maire—embrace him of both arms.

That was in Simla. All things are possible in Simla.

Even embraces.

His wife! Mon Dieu, his wife!

The aheuried imagination prostrates itself at the remembrance of the splendours Orientals of the Lady Cyril—the very respectable the Lady Wollobie.

That was in Simla. All things are possible in Simla. Even wives. In those days I was—what you call—a Schnobb. I am now a much larger Schnobb. Voila the only difference. Thus it is true that travel expands the mind.

But let us return to our Wollobies.

I admired that man there with the both hands. I crawled before the Lady Wollobie—platonically. The man the most brave would be only platonic towards that lady. And I was also afraid. Subsequently I went to a dance. The wine equalled not the splendour of the Wollobies. Nor the food. But there was upon the floor an open space—large and park-like. It protected the dignity Wollobicallisme. It was guarded by Aides-de-Camp. With blue silk in their coat-tails—turned up. With pink eyes and white moustaches to ravish. Also turned up.

To me addressed himself an Aide-de-Camp.

That was in Simla. To-day I do not speak to Aides-de-Camp.

I confine myself exclusively to the cabdrivaire. He does not know so much bad language, but he can drive better.

I approached, under the protection of the Aide-de-Camp, the luminosity of Sir Wollobie.

The world entire regarded.

The band stopped. The lights burned blue. A domestic dropped a plate.

It was an inspiring moment.

From the summit of Jakko forty-five monkeys looked down upon the crisis.

Sir Wollobie spoke.

To me in that expanse of floor cultured and park-like. He said: "I have long desired to make your acquaintance."

The blood bouilloned in my head. I became pink. I was aneantied under the weight of an embarras insubrimable.

At that moment Sir Wollobie became oblivious of my personality. That was his custom.

Wiping my face upon my coat-tails I refugied myself among the foules.

I had been spoken to by Sir Wollobie. That was in Simla. That also is history.

Pass now several years. To the day before yesterday!

This also is history—farcical, immense, tragi-comic, but true.

Know you the Totnam Cortrode?

Here lives Maple, who sells washing appliances and tables of exotic legs.

Here voyages also a Omnibuse Proletariat.

That is to say for One penny.

Two pence is the refined volupte of the Aristocrat.

I am of the people.

Entre nous the connection is not desired by us. The people address to me epithets, entirely unprintable. I reply that they should wash. The situation is strained. Hence the Strike Docks and the Demonstrations Laborious.

Upon the funeste tumbril of the Proletariat I take my seat.

I demand air outside upon the roof.

I will have all my penny.

The tumbril advances.

A man aged loses his equilibrium and deposits himself into my lap.

Following the custom of the Brutal Londoner I demand the Devil where he shoves himself.

He apologises supplicatorically.

I grunt.

Encore the tumbril shakes herself.

I appropriate the desired seat of the old man.

The conductaire cries to loud voice: "Fare, Guvnor."

He produces one penny.

A reminiscence phantasmal provokes itself.

I beat him on the back.

It is Sir Wollobie; the ex-Everything!

Also the ex-Eveiything else!

Figure you the situation!

He clasps my hand.

As a child clasps the hand of its nurse.

He demands of me particular rensignments of my health. It is to him a matter important.

Other time he regulated the health of forty-five millions.

I riposte. I enquire of his liver—his pancreas, his abdomen.

The sacred internals of Sir Wollobie!

He has them all. And they all make him ill.

He is very lonely. He speaks of his wife. There is no Lady Wollobie, but a woman in a flat in Bayswater who cries in her sleep for more curricles.

He does not say this, but I understand.

He derides the Council of the Indian Office. He imprecates the Government.

He curses the journals.

He has a clob. He curses that clob.

Females with teeth monstrous explain to him the theory of Government.

Men of long hair, the psychologues of the paint-pots, correct him tenderly, but from above.

He has known of the actualities of life—Death, Power, Responsibility, Honour—the Good accomplished, the effacement of Wrong for forty years.

There remains to him a seat in a penny 'bus.

If I do not take him from that.

I rap my heels on the knife-board. I sing "tra la la" I am also well disposed to larmes.

He courbes himself underneath an ulstaire and he damns the fog to eternity.

He wills not that I leave him. He desires that I come to dinner.

I am grave. I think upon Lady Wollobie—shorn of chaprassies—at the Clob. Not in Bayswater.

I accept. He will bore me affreusely, but . . . I have taken his seat.

He descends from the tumbril of his humiliation, and the street hawker rolls a barrow up his waistcoat.

Then intervenes the fog—dense, impenetrable, hopeless, without end.

It is because of the fog that there is a drop upon the end of my nose so chiselled.

Gentlemen the Governors, the Lieutenant-Governors and the Commissaires, behold the doom prepared.

I am descended to the gates of your Life in Death. Which is Brompton or Bayswater.

You do not believe? You will try the constituencies when you return; is it not so?

You will fail. As others failed.

Your seat waits you on the top of an Omnibuse Proletariat.

I shall be there.

You will embrace me as a shipwrecked man embraces a log. You will be "dam glad t' see me."

I shall grin.

Oh Life! Oh Death! Oh Power! Oh Toil! Oh Hope! Oh Stars! Oh Honour! Oh Lodgings! Oh Fog! Oh Omnibuses! Oh Despair! Oh Skittles!

Griffiths the Safe Man

As the title indicates, this story deals with the safeness of Griffiths the safe man, the secure person, the reliable individual, the sort of man you would bank with. I am proud to write about Griffiths, for I owe him a pleasant day. This story is dedicated to my friend Griffiths, the remarkably trustworthy mortal.

In the beginning there were points about Griffiths. He quoted proverbs. A man who quotes proverbs is confounded by proverbs. He is also confounded by his friends. But I never confounded Griffths—not even in that supreme moment when the sweat stood on his brow in agony and his teeth were fixed like bayonets and he swore horribly. Even then, I say, I sat on my own trunk, the trunk that opened, and told Griffiths that I had always respected him, but never more than at the present moment. He was so safe, y' know.

Safeness is a matter of no importance to me. If my trunk won't lock when I jump on it thrice, I strap it up and go on to something else. If my carpet-bag is too full, I let the tails of shirts and the ends of ties bubble over and go down the street with the affair. It all comes right in the end, and if it does not, what is a man that he should fight against Fate?

But Griffiths is not constructed in that manner. He says: "Safe bind is safe find." That, rather, is what he used to say. He has seen reason to alter his views. Everything about Griffiths is safe—entirely safe. His trunk is locked by two hermetical gun-metal double-end Chubbs; his bedding-roll opens to a letter padlock capable of two million combinations; his hat-box has a lever patent safety on it; and the grief of his life is that he cannot lock up the ribs of his umbrella safely. If you could get at his soul you would find it ready strapped up and labelled for heaven. That is Griffiths.

When we went to Japan together, Griffiths kept all his money under lock and key. I carried mine in my coat-tail pocket. But all Griffiths' contraptions did not prevent him from spending exactly as much as I did. You see, when he had worried his way through the big strap, and the little strap, and the slide-valve, and the spring lock, and the key that turned twice and a quarter, he felt as though he had earned any money he found, whereas I could get masses of sinful wealth by merely pulling out my handkerchief— dollars and five dollars and ten dollars, all mixed up with the tobacco or flying down the road. They looked much too pretty to spend.

"Safe bind, safe find," said Griffiths in the treaty port.

He never really began to lock things up severely till we got our passports to travel upcountry. He took charge of mine for me, on the ground that I was an imbecile. As you are asked for your passport at every other shop, all the hotels, most of the places of amusement, and on the top of each hill, I got to appreciate Griffiths' self-sacrifice. He would be biting a strap with his teeth or calculating the combinations of his padlocks among a ring of admiring Japanese while I went for a walk into the interior.

"Safe bind, safe find," said Griffiths. That was true, because I was bound to find Griffiths somewhere near his beloved keys and straps. He never seemed to see that half the pleasure of his trip was being strapped and keyed out of him.

We never had any serious difficulty about the passports in the whole course of our wanderings. What I purpose to describe now is merely an incident of travel. It had no effect on myself, but it nearly broke Griffiths' heart.

We were travelling from Kyoto to Otsu along a very dusty road full of pretty girls. Every time I stopped to play with one of them Griffiths grew impatient. He had telegraphed for rooms at the only hotel in Otsu, and was afraid that there would be no accommodation. There were only three rooms in the hotel, and "Safe bind, safe find," said Griffiths. He was telegraphing ahead for something.

Our hotel was three-quarters Japanese and one-quarter European. If you walked across it it shook, and if you laughed the roof fell off. Strange Japanese came in and dined with you, and Jap maidens looked through the windows of the bathroom while you were bathing.

We had hardly put the luggage down before the proprietor asked for our passports. He asked me of all people in the world. "I have the passports," said Griffiths with pride. "They are in the yellow-hide bag. Turn it very carefully on to the right side, my good man. You have no such locks in Japan, I'm quite certain." Then he knelt down and brought out a bunch of keys as big as his fist. You must know that every Japanese carries a little belaiti-made handbag with nickel fastenings. They take an interest in handbags.

"Safe bind, safe—Damn the key! What's wrong with it?" said Griffiths.

The hotel proprietor bowed and smiled very politely for at least five minutes, Griffiths crawling over and mider and round and about his bag the while, "It's a percussating compensator," said he, half to himself. "I've never known a percussating compensator do this before." He was getting heated and red in the face.

"Key stuck, eh? I told you those fooling little spring locks are sure to go wrong sooner or later."

"Fooling little devils. It's a percussating comp—There goes the key. Now it won't move either way. I'll give you the passport to-morrow. Passport kul demang manana—catchee in a little time. Won't that do for you?"

Griffiths was getting really angry. The proprietor was more polite than ever. He bowed and left the room. "That's a good little chap," said Griffiths. "Now we'll settle down and see what the mischief's wrong with this bag. You catch one end."

"Not in the least," I said. "'Safe bind, safe find,' You did the binding. How can you expect me to do the finding? I'm an imbecile unfit to be trusted with a passport, and now I'm going for a walk." The Japanese are really the politest nation in the world. When the hotel proprietor returned with a policeman he did ppt at once thrust the man on Griffiths' notice. He put him in the verandah and let him clank his sword gently once or twice.

"Little chap's brought a blacksmith," said Griffiths, but when he saw the policeman his face became ugly. The policeman came into the room and tried to assist. Have you ever seen a four-foot policeman in white cotton gloves and a stand-up collar lunging percussating compensator look with a five-foot sword? I enjoyed the sight for a few minutes before I went out to look at Otsu, which is a nice town. No one hindered me. Griffiths was so completely the head of the firm that had I set the town on fire he would have been held responsible.

I went to a temple, and a policeman said "passport." I said, "The other gentleman has got. "Where is other gentleman?" said the policeman, syllable by syllable, in the Ollendorfian style. "In the ho-tel," said I; and he waddled off to catch him. It seemed to me that I could do a great deal towards cheering Griffiths all alone in his bedroom with that wicked bad lock, the hotel proprietor, the policeman, the room-boy, and the girl who helped one to bathe. With this idea I stood in front of four policemen, and they all asked for my passport and were all sent to the hotel, syllable by syllable—I mean one by one.

Some soldiers of the 9th N, I. were strolling about the streets, and they were idle. It is unwise to let a soldier be idle. He may get drunk. When the fourth policeman said: "Where is other gentleman?" I said: "In the hotel, and take soldiers—those soldiers."

"How many soldiers?" said the policeman firmly.

"Take all soldiers," I said. There were four files in the street just then. The policeman spoke to them, and they caught up their big sword-bayonets, nearly as long as themselves, and waddled after him.

I followed them, but first I bought some sweets and gave one to a child. That was enough. Long before I had reached the hotel I had a tail of fifty babies. These I seduced into the long passage that ran through the house, and then I slid the grating that answers to the big hall-door. That house was full—pit, boxes and galleries—for Griffiths had created an audience of his own, and I also had not been idle.

The four files of soldiers and the five policemen were marking time on the boards of Griffith's room, while the landlord and the landlord's wife, and the two scullions, and the bath-girl, and the cook-boy, and the boy who spoke English, and the boy who didn't, and the boy who tried to, and the cook, filled all the space that wasn't devoted to babies asking the foreigner for more sweets.

Somewhere in the centre of the mess was Griffiths and a yellow-hide bag. I don't think he had looked up once since I left, for as he raised his eyes at my voice I heard him cry: "Good heavens! are they going to train the guns of the city on me? What's the meaning of the regiment? I'm a British subject."

"What are you looking for?" I asked.

"The passports—your passports—the double-dyed passports! Oh, give a man room to use his arms. Get me a hatchet."

"The passports, the passports!" I said. "Have you looked in your great-coat? It's on the bed, and there's a blue envelope in it that looks like a passport. You put it there before you left Kyoto."

Griffiths looked. The landlord looked. The landlord took the passport and bowed. The five policemen bowed and went out one by one; the 9th N. I. formed fours and went out; the household bowed, and there was a long silence. Then the bath-girl began to giggle.

When Griffiths wanted to speak to me I was on the other side of the regiment of children in the passage, and he had time to reflect before he could work his way through them.

They formed his guard-of -honour when he took the bag to the locksmith.

I abode on the mountains of Otsu till dinnertime.

It!

There was no talk of it for a fortnight. We spoke of latitude and longitude and the proper manufacture of sherry cobblers, while the steamer cut open a glassy-smooth sea. Then we turned towards China and drank farewell to the nearer East. "We shall reach Hongkong without being it," said the nervous lady.

"Nobody of ordinary strength of mind ever was it," said the big fat man with the voice. I kept my eye on the big fat man. He boasted too much.

The China seas are governed neither by wind nor calm. Deep down under the sapphire waters sits a green and yellow devil who suffers from indigestion perpetually. When he is unwell he troubles the waters above with his twistings and writhings. Thus it happens that it is never calm in the China seas.

The sun was shining brightly when the big fat man with the voice came up the companion and looked at the horizon.

"Hah!" said he, "calm as ditch water! Now I remember when I was in the Florida in '80, meeting a tidal-wave that turned us upside down for five minutes, and most of the people inside out, by Jove!" He expatiated at length on the heroism displayed by himself when "even the Captain was down, sir!"

I said nothing, but I kept my eyes upon the strong man.

The Sun continued to shine brightly, and it also kept an eye in the same direction. I went to the far-off fo'c'sle, where the sheep and the cow and the bo'sun and the second-class passengers dwell together in amity. "Bo'sun," said I, "how's her head?"

"Direckly in front of her, sir," replied that ill-mannered soul, "but we shall be meetin' a head-sea in half an hour that'll put your head atween of your legs. Go aft an' tell that to them first-class passengers."

I went aft, but I said nothing. We went, later, to tiffin, and there was a fine funereal smell of stale curries and tinned meats in the air. Conversation was animated, for most of the passengers had been together for five weeks and had developed two or three promising flirtations. I was a stranger—a minnow among Tritons—a third man in the cabin. Only those who have been a third man in the cabin know what this means. Suddenly and without warning our ship curtsied. It was neither a bob nor a duck nor a lurch, but a long, sweeping, stately old-fashioned curtsy. Followed a lull in the conversation. I was distinctly conscious that I had left my stomach two feet in the air, and waited for the return roll to join it. "Prettily the old hooper rides, doesn't she?" said the strong man. "I hope she won't do it often," said the pretty lady with the changing complexion.

"Wha-hoop! Wha—wha—wha—willy whoop!" said the screw, that had managed to come out of the water and was racing wildly.

"Good heavens! is the ship going down?" said the fat lady, clutching her own private claret bottle that she might not die athirst. The ship went down at the word—with a drunken lurch down she went, and a smothered yell from one of the cabins showed that there was water in the sea. The portholes closed with a clash, and we rose and fell on the swell of the bo'sun's head-sea. The conversation died out. Some complained that the saloon was stuffy, and fled upstairs to the deck. The strong man brought up the rear.

"Ooshy—ooshy—wooshy—woggle wop!' cried a big wave without a head. "Get up, old girl" and he smacked the ship most disrespectfully under the counter, and she squirmed as she took the drift of the next sea.

"She—ah—rides very prettily," repeated the strong man as the companion stairs spumed him from them and he wound his arms round the nearest steward.

"Damn prettily," said the necked officer. "I'm going to lie down. Never could stand the China seas,"

"Most refreshing thing in the world," said the strong man faintly.

I took counsel purely with myself, which is to say, my stomach, and perceived that the worst would not befall me.

"Come to the fo'c'sle, then, and feel the wind," said I to the strong man. The plover's egg eyes of three yellowish-green girls were upon him.

"With pleasure," said he, and I bore him away to where the cut-water was pulling up the scared flying-fishes as a spaniel flushes game. In front of us was the illimitable blue, lightly ridged by the procession of the big blind rollers. Up rose the stem till six feet of the red paint stood clear above the blue—from twenty-three feet to eighteen I could count as I leaned over. Then the sapphire crashed into splintered crystal with a musical jar, and the white spray licked the anchor channels as we drove down and down, sucking at the sea. I kept my eye upon the strong man, and I noticed that his mouth was slightly open, the better to inhale the rushing wind. When I looked a second time he was gone. The driven spray was scarcely quicker in its flight. My excellent stomach behaved with temperance and chastity. I enjoyed the fo'c'sle, and my delight was the greater when I reflected on the strong man. Unless I was much mistaken, he would know all about it in half an hour.

I went aft, and a lull between two waves heard the petulant pop of a champagne cork. No one drinks champagne after tiffin except . . . It.

The strong man had ordered the champagne. There were bottles of it flying about the quarter-deck. The engaged couple were sipping it out of one glass, but their faces were averted like our parents of old. They were ashamed.

"You may go! You may go to Hongkong for me!" shouted half-a-dozen little waves together, pulling the ship several ways at once. She rolled stately, and from that moment settled down to the work of the evening. I cannot blame her, for I am sure she did not know her own strength. It didn't hurt her to be on her side, and play cat-and-mouse, and puss-in-the corner, and hide-and-seek, but it destroyed the passengers. One by one they sank into long chairs and gazed at the sky. But even there the little white moved, and there was not one stable thing in heaven above or the waters beneath. My virtuous and very respectable stomach behaved with integrity and resolution. I treated it to a gin cocktail, which I sucked by the side of the strong man, who told me in confidence that he had been overcome by the sun at the fo'c'sle. Sun fever does not make people cold and clammy and blue. I sat with him and tried to make him talk about the Florida and his voyages in the past. He evaded me and went down below. Three minutes later I followed him with a thick cheroot. Into his bunk I went, for I knew he would be helpless. He was—he was—he was. He wallowed supine, and I stood in the doorway smoking.

"What is it?" said I.

He wrestled with his pride—his wicked pride—but he would not tell a lie.

"It," said he. And it was so.

The rolling continues. The ship is a shambles, and I have six places on each side of me all to myself.

A Fallen Idol

Will the public be good enough to look into this business? It has sent Crewe to bed, and Mottleby is applying for home leave, and I've lost my faith in man altogether, and the Club gives it up. Trivey is the only man who is unaffected by the catastrophe, and he says "I told you so." We were all proud of Trivey at the Club, and would have crowned him with wreaths of Bougainvillea had he permitted the liberty. But Trivey was an austere man. The utmost that he permitted himself to say was: "I can stretch a little bit when I'm in the humour." We called him the Monumental Liar. Nothing that the Club offered was too good for Trivey. He had the soft chair opposite the thermantidote in the hot weather, and he made up his own four at whist. When visitors came in—globe-trotters for choice—Trivey used to unmuzzle himself and tell tales that sent the globe-trotter out of the Club on tiptoe looking for snakes in his hat and tigers in the compound. Whenever a man from a strange Club came in Trivey used to call for a whisky and ginger-wine and rout that man on all points—from horses upward. There was a man whose nickname was "Ananias," who came from the Prince's Plungers to look at Trivey; and, though Trivey was only a civilian, the Plunger man resigned his title to the nickname before eleven o'clock. He made it over to Trivey on a card, and Trivey hung up the concession in his quarters. We loved Trivey—all of us; and now we don't love him any more.

A man from the frontier came in and began to tell tales—some very good ones, and some better than good. He was an outsider, but he had a wonderful imagination—for the frontier. He told six stories before Trivey brought up his first line, and three more before Trivey hurled his reserves into the fray.

"When I was at Anungaracharlupillay in Madras," said Trivey quietly, "there was a rogue elephant cutting about the district. And I came upon him asleep." All the Club stopped talking here, until Trivey had finished the story. He told us that he, in the company of another man, had found the rogue asleep, but just as they got up to the brute's head it woke up with a scream. Then Trivey, who was careful to explain that he was a "bit powerful about the arms," caught hold of its ears as it rose, and hung there, kicking the animal in the eyes, which so bewildered it that it stayed screaming and frightened until Trivey's ally shot it behind the shoulder, and the villagers ran in and hamstrung it. It evidently died from loss of blood. Trivey was hanging on the ears and kicking hard for nearly fifteen minutes. When the frontier man heard the story he put his hands in front of his face and sobbed audibly. We gave him all the drinks he wanted, and he recovered sufficiently to carry away eighty rupees at whist later on; but his nerve was irretrievably shattered. He will be no use on the frontier any more. The rest of the Club were very pleased with Trivey, because these frontier men, and especially the guides, want a great deal of keeping in order. Trivey was quite modest. He was a truly great soul, and popular applause never turned his head. As I have said, we loved Trivey, till that fatal day when Crewe announced that he had been transferred for a couple of months to Animgaracharlupillay. "Oh!" said Trivey, "I dare say they'll remember about my rogue elephant down there. You ask 'em, Crewe." Then we felt sorry for Trivey, because we were sure that he was arriving at that stage of mental decay when a man begins to believe in his own fictions. That spoils a man's hand. Crewe wrote up once or twice to Mottleby, saying that he would bring back a story that would make our hair curl. Good stories are scarce in Madras, and we rather scoffed at the announcement. When Crewe returned it was easy to see that he was bursting with importance. He gave a big dinner at the Club and invited nearly everybody but Trivey, who went off after dinner to teach a young subaltern to play "snooker." At coffee and cheroots, Crewe could not restrain himself any longer. "I say, you Johnnies, it's all true—every single word of it—and you can throw the decanter at my head and I'll apologise. The whole village was full of it. There was a rogue elephant, and it slept, and Trivey did catch hold of its ears and kick it in the eyes, and hang on for ten minutes, at least, and all the rest of it. I neglected my regular work to sift that story, and on my honour the tale's an absolute fact. The headsman said so, all the shikaries said so, and all the villages corroborated it. Now would a whole village volunteer a lie that would do them no good?" You might have heard a cigar-ash fall after this statement. Then Mottleby said, with deep disgust: "What can you do with a man like that? His best and brightest lie, too!" "'t'isn't!" shrieked Crewe. "It's a fact—a nickel-plated, teak-wood, Tantalusaction, forty-five rupee fact." "That only makes it worse," said Mottleby; and we all felt that was true. We ran into the billiard-room to talk to Trivey, but he said we had put him off his stroke; and that was all the satisfaction we got out of him. Later on he repeated that he was a "bit powerful about the arms," and went to bed. We sat up half the night devising vengeance on Trivey. We were very angry, and there was no hope of hushing up the tale. The man had taken us in completely, and now that we've lost our champion Ananias, all the frontier will laugh at us, and we shall never be able to trust a word that Trivey says.

I ask with Mottleby: "What can you do with a man like that?"

New Brooms

"If seven maids with seven mops
Swept it for half a year,
Do you suppose," the Walrus said,
"That they could sweep it clear?"

Ram buksh, Aryan, went to bed with his buffalo, five goats, three children and a wife, because the evening mists were chilly. His hut was builded on the mud scooped from a green and smelly tank, and there were microbes in the thin blood of Ram Buksh.

Ram Buksh went to bed on a charpoy stretched across the blue tepid drain, because the nights were hot; and there were more microbes in his blood. Then the rains came, and Ram Buksh paddled, mid-thigh deep, in water for a day or two with his buffaloes till he was aware of a crampsome feeling at the pit of his stomach. "Mother of my children," said Ram Buksh, "this is death." They gave him cardamoms and capsicums, and gingelly-oil and cloves, and they prayed for him. "It is enough," said Ram Buksh, and he twisted himself into a knot and died, and they burned him slightly—for the wood was damp—and the rest of him floated down the river, and was caught in an undercurrent at the bank, and there stayed; and when Imam Din, the Jeweller, drank of the stream five days later, he drank Lethe, and passed away, crying in vain upon his gods. His family did not report his death to the Municipality, for they desired to keep Imam Din with them. Therefore, they buried him under the flagging in the courtyard, secretly and by night. Twelve days later, Imam Din had made connection with the well of the house, and there was typhus among the women in the zenana, but no one knew anything about it—some died and some did not; and Ari Booj, the Faquir, added to the interest of the proceedings by joining the funeral procession and distributing gratis the more malignant forms of smallpox, from which he was just recovering. He had come all the way from Delhi, and had slept on no less than fifteen different charpoys; and that was how they got the smallpox into Bahadurgarh. But Eshmith Sahib's Dhobi picked it up from An Booj when Imam Din's wife was being buried—for he was a merry man, and sent home a beautiful sample among the Sunday shirts. So Eshmith Sahib died.

He was only a link in the chain which crawled from the highest to the lowest. The wonder was not that men died like sheep, but that they did not die like flies; for their lives and their surroundings, their deaths, were part of a huge conspiracy against cleanliness. And the people loved to have it so. They huddled together in frowsy clusters, while Death mowed his way through them till the scythe blunted against the unresisting flesh, and he had to get a new one. They died by fever, tens of thousands in a month; they died by cholera a thousand in a week; they died of smallpox, scores in the mohulla, and by dysentery by tens in a house; and when all other deaths failed they laid them down and died because their hands were too weak to hold on to life.

To and fro stamped the Englishman, who is everlastingly at war with the scheme of things. "You shall not die," he said, and he decreed that there should be no more famines. He poured grain down their throats, and when all failed he went down into the strife and died with them, swearing, and toiling, and working till the last. He fought the famine and put it to flight. Then he wiped his forehead, and attacked the pestilence that walketh in the darkness. Death's scythe swept to and fro, around and about him; but he only planted his feet more firmly in the way of it, and fought off Death with a dog-whip. "Live, you ruffian!" said the Englishman to Ram Buksh as he rode through the reeking village. "Jenab!" said Ram Buksh, "it is as it was in the days of our fathers!" "Then stand back while I alter it," said the Englishman; and by force, and cunning, and a brutal disregard of vested interests, he strove to keep Ram Buksh alive. "Clean your mohullas; pay for clean water; keep your streets swept; and see that your food is sound, or I'll make your life a burden to you," said the Englishman. Sometimes he died; but more often Ram Buksh went down, and the Englishman regarded each death as a personal insult.

"Softly, there!" said the Government of India. "You're twisting his tail. You mustn't do that. The spread of education forbids, and Ram Buksh is an intelligent voter. Let him work out his own salvation."

"H'm!" said the Englishman with his head in a midden; "collectively you always were a fool. Here, Ram Buksh, the Sirkar says you are to do all these things for yourself."

"Jenab!" says Ram Buksh, and fell to breeding microbes with renewed vigour.

Curiously enough, it was in the centres of enlightenment that he prosecuted his experiments most energetically. The education had been spread, but so thinly that it could not disguise Ram Buksh's natural instincts. He created an African village, and said it was the hub of the universe, and all the dirt of all the roads failed to convince him that he was not the most advanced person in the world. There was a pause, and Ram Buksh got himself fearfully entangled among Boards and Committees, but he valued them as a bowerbird values shells and red rags. "See!" said the Englishman to the Government of India, "he is blind on that side—blind by birth, training, instinct and associations. Five-sixths of him is poor stock raised off poor soil, and he'll die on the least provocation. You've no right to let him kill himself."

"But he's educated," said the Government of India.

"I'll concede everything," said the Englishman. "He's a statesman, author, poet, politician, artist, and all else that you wish him to be, but he isn't a Sanitary Engineer. And while you're training him he is dying. Goodness knows that my share in the Government is very limited nowadays, but I'm willing to do all the work while he gets all the credit if you'll only let me have some authority over him in his mud-pie making,"

"But the liberty of the subject is sacred," said the Government of India.

"I haven't any," said the Englishman. "He can trail through my compounds; start shrines in the public roads; poison my family; have me in court for nothing; ruin my character; spend my money, and call me an assassin when all is done. I don't object. Let me look after his sanitation."

"But the days of a paternal Government are over; we must depend on the people. Think of what they would say at home," said the Government of India. "We have issued a resolution—indeed we have!"

The Englishman sat down and groaned. "I believe you'll issue a resolution some day notifying your own abolition," said he. "What are you going to do?"

"Constitute more Boards," said the Government of India. "Boards of Control and Supervision—Fund Boards—all sorts of Boards. Nothing like system. It will be at work in three years or so. We haven't any money, but that's a detail."

The Englishman looked at the resolution and sniffed. "It doesn't touch the weak point of the country."

"What will touch the weak point of the country, then?" said the Government of India.

"I used to," said the Englishman. "I was the District Officer, and I twisted their tails. You have taken away my power, and now—"

"Well," said the Government of India, "you seem to think a good deal of yourself."

"Never mind me," said the Englishman. "I'm an effete relic of the past. But Ram Buksh will die, as he used to do."

And now we all wait to see which is right.

Tiglath Pileser

Thank Heaven he is dead! The municipality sent a cart and a man only this morning, and, all the servants aiding with ropes and tackle, the carcase of Tiglath was borne away—a wobbling lump. His head was thrust over the tailboard of the cart. Upon it was stamped an expression of horror and surprise, unutterable and grotesque. I have put away my rifle, I have cheered my heart with wine, and I sit down now to write the story of Tiglath, the Utter Brute. His own kind, alas! will not read it, and thus it will be shorn of instruction; but owners will kindly take notice, and when it pleases Heaven to inflict them with such an animal as Tiglath they will know what to do. To begin with, I bought him, his vices thick as his barsati, for a hundred and seventy rupees, a five-chambered, muzzle-loading revolver, and a Cawnpore saddle.

"Of course, for that price," said Staveley, you can't expect everything. He's not what one would call absolutely sound, y' know, but there's no end of work in him, and if you only give him the butt he'll go like a steam-engine."

"Staveley," I answered, "when you admit that he is not perfection I perceive that I am in for a really Good Thing. Don't hurt your conscience, Staveley. Tell me what is his chief vice—weakness, partiality—anything you choose to call it. I shall get to know the minor defects in the course of nature; but what is Tiglath's real shouk?"

Staveley reflected a moment. "Well, really, I can't quite say, old man, straight off the reel, y' know. He's a oner to go when his head's turned to home. He's a regular feeder, and vaseline will cure that little eruption"—with its malignant barsati—"in no time. Oh, I forgot his shouk: I don't know exactly how to describe it, but he yaws a good deal," said Staveley.

"He how muches?" I asked.

"Yaws," said Staveley; "goes a bit wide upon occasions, but a good coachwan will cure that in one drive. My man let him do what he liked. One fifty and a hundred, ten and ten is twenty—one-seventy. Many thanks, indeed. I'll send over his bedding and ropes. He's a powerful upstanding horse, though rather picked up just at present."

Staveley departed, and I was left alone with Tiglath. I called him Tiglath because he resembled a lathy pig. Later on I called him Pileser on account of his shouk; but my coachwan, a strong, masterless man, called him "haramzada chor, shaitan ké bap" and "oont ki beta" He certainly was a powerful horse, being full fifteen-two at the withers, with the girth of a waler, and at first the docility of an Arab. There was something wrong with his feet—permanently—but he was a considerate beast, and never had more than one leg in hospital at a time. The other three were still movable, and Tiglath never grudged them in my service. I write this in justice to his memory; the creaking of the wheels of the municipal cart being still in my ears.

For a season—some twelve days—Tiglath was beyond reproach. He had not a cheerful disposition, nor did his pendulous underlip add to his personal beauty; but he made no complaints, and moved swiftly to and from office. The hot weather gave place to the cool breezes of October, and with the turn of the year the slumbering devil in the soul of Tiglath spread its wings and crowed aloud. I fed him well, I had aided his barsati, I had lapped his lame legs in thanda putties, and adorned his sinful body with new harness. He rewarded me upon a day with an exhibition so new and strange that I feared for the moment his reason had been unhinged. Slowly, with a malevolent grin, Tiglath, the pampered, turned at right angles to the carriage—a newly-varnished one—and backed the front wheels up the verandah steps, letting them down with a bump. He then wheeled round and round in the portico, and all but brought the carriage over. The show lasted for ten minutes, at the end of which time he trotted peacefully away.

I was pained and grieved—nothing more, upon my honour. I forbade the sais to kick Tiglath in the stomach, for I was persuaded that the harness galled him, and, in this belief, at the end of the day, undressed him tenderly and fitted sheepskin all over the said harness. Tiglath ate the sheepskin next day, and I did not renew it.

A week later I met the Judge. It was a purely accidental interview. I would have avoided it, as the Judge and I did not love each other, but the shafts of my carriage were through the circular front of his brougham, and Tiglath was rubbing the boss of his headstall tenderly against the newly-varnished panels of the same. The Judge complained that he might have been impaled as he sat. My coachwan declared on oath that the horse deliberately ran into the brougham. Tiglath tendered no evidence, and I began to mistrust him.

At the end of a month I perceived that my friends and acquaintances avoided me markedly. The appearance of Tiglath at the bandstand was enough to clear a space of ten yards in my immediate neighbourhood. I had to shout to my friends from afar, and they shouted back the details of the little bills which I had to pay their coach-builders. Tiglath was suffering from carriagecidal mania, and the coachwan had asked for leave. "Stay with me, Ibrahim," I said. "Thou seest how the sahib log do now avoid us. Get a new and a stout chabuq, and instruct Tiglath in the paths of straight walking."

"He will smash the Heaven-born's carriage. He is an old and stale devil, but in this matter extreme wise," answered Ibrahim. "Kitto sahib's filton hath he smashed, and Burkitt sahib's brougham gharri, and another tim-tum, and Staveley sahib's carriage is still being mended. What profit is this horse? He feigns blindness and much fear, and in the guise of innocency works evil. I will stay, sahib, but the blood of this thy new carriage be upon the brute's head and not upon mine own."

I have no space to describe the war of the next few weeks. Foiled in his desire to ruin only neighbours' property, Tiglath fell back literally, upon his own—my carriage. He tried the verandah step trick till he bent the springs, and wheeled round till the turning action grew red-hot; he scraped stealthily by walls; he performed between heavy-laden bullock-trains, but his chief delight was a pas de fantasie on a dark night and a high, level road. Yet what he did he did staidly and without heat, as without remorse. He was vetted thrice, and his eyes were pronounced sound. After this information I laid my bones to the battle, and acquired a desperate facility of leaping from the carriage and kicking Tiglath on the stomach as soon as he wheeled around; leaping back at the risk of my life when he set off at full speed. I pressed the lighted end of a cheroot just behind the collar-buckle; I applied fusees to those flaccid nostrils, and I beat him about the head with a stick continually. It was necessary, but it was also demoralising. A year of Tiglath would have converted me into a cold-blooded vivisectionist, or a native bullock-driver. Each day I took stock of the injuries to my carriage. I had long since given up all hope of keeping it in decent repair; and each day I devised fresh torments for Tiglath.

He never meant to injure himself, I am certain, and no one was more astonished than he when he backed on the Balmnon road, and dropped the carriage into a nullah on the night of the Jamabundi Moguls' dance. I did not go to the dance. I was bent considerably, and one side of the coachwan's face was flayed. When he had pieced the wreck together, he only said, "Sahib!" and I said only "Bohat acha." But we each knew what the other meant. Next mom Tiglath was stiflf and strained. I gave him time to recover and to enjoy life. When I heard him squealing to the grass-cutter's ponies I knew that the hour had come. I ordered the carriage, and myself superintended the funeral toilet of Tiglath. His harness brasses shone like gold, his coat like a bottle, and he lifted his feet daintily. Had he even then, at the eleventh hour, given promise of amendment, I should have held my hand. But as I entered the carriage I saw the hunching of his quarters that presaged trouble. "Go forward, Tiglath, my love, my pride, my delight," I murmured. "For a surety it is a matter of life and death this day." The sais ran to his head with a fragment of chupatti, saved from his all too scanty rations; the man loved him. And Tiglath swung round to the left in the portico; round and round swung he, till the near ear touched the muzzle of the shot-gun that waited its coming. He never flinched; he pressed his fate. The coachwan threw down the reins as, with four ounces of No. 5 shot behind the hollow of the root of the ear, Tiglath fell. In his death he accomplished the desire of his life, for he fell upon the shaft and broke it into three pieces. I looked on him as he lay, and of a sudden the reason of the horror in his eyes was made clear. Tiglath, the breaker of carriages, the strong, the rebellious, had passed into the shadowy spirit land, where there was nought to destroy and no power to destroy it with. The ghastly foreknowledge of the flitting soul was written on the glazing eyeball.

I repented me, then, that I had slain Tiglath, for I had no intention of punishing him in the hereafter.

The Likes o' Us

It was the General Officer Commanding, riding down the Mall, on the Arab with the perky tail, and he condescended to explain some of the mysteries of his profession. But the point on which he dwelt most pompously was the ease with which the Private Thomas Atkins could be "handled," as he called it. "Only feed him and give him a little work to do, and you can do anything with him," said the General Officer Commanding. "There's no refinement about Tommy, you know; and one is very like another. They've all the same ideas and traditions and prejudices. They're all big children. Fancy any man in his senses shooting about these hills." There was the report of a shot-gun in the valley. "I suppose they've hit a dog. Happy as the day is long when they're out shooting dogs. Just like a big child is Tommy," He touched up his horse and cantered away. There was a sound of angry voices down the hillside.

"All right, you soor—I won't never forget this—mind you, not as long as I live, and s' 'elp me—I'll—" The sentence finished in what could be represented by a blaze of asterisks.

A deeper voice cut it short: "Oh, no, you won't, neither! Look a-here, you young smitcher. If I was to take yer up now, and knock off your 'ead again' that tree, could ye say anythin'? No, nor yet do anythin'. If I was to—Ah! you would, would you? There!" Some one had evidently sat down with a thud, and was swearing nobly. I slid over the edge of the khud, down through the long grass, and fetched up, after the manner of a sledge, with my feet in the broad of the back of Gunner Barnabas in the Mountain Battery, my friend, the very strong man. He was sitting upon a man—a khaki-coloured volcano of blasphemy— and was preparing to smoke. My sudden arrival threw him off his balance for a moment. Then, readjusting his chair, he bade me good-day.

"'Im an' me 'ave bin 'avin' an argument," said Gunner Barnabas placidly. "I was going for to half kill him an' 'eave 'im into the bushes 'ere, but, seein' that you 'ave come, sir, and very welcome when you do come, we will 'ave a court-martial instead. Shacklock, are you willin'?" The volcano, who had been swearing uninterruptedly through this oration, expressed a desire, in general and particular terms, to see Gimner Barnabas in Torment and the "civilian" on the next gridiron.

Private Shacklock was a tow-haired, scrofulous boy of about two-and-twenty. His nose was bleeding profusely, and the live air attested that he had been drinking quite as much as was good for him. He lay, stomach-down, on a little level spot on the hillside; for Gunner Barnabas was sitting between his shoulderblades, and his was not a weight to wriggle under. Private Shacklock could barely draw breath to swear, but he did the best that in him lay. "Amen," said Gunner Barnabas piously, when an unusually brilliant string of oaths came to an end. "Seein' that this gentleman 'ere has never seen the inside o' the orsepitals you've gotten in, and the clinks you've been chucked into like a hay-bundle, per-haps, Privite Shacklock, you will stop. You are a-makin' of 'im sick." Private Shacklock said that he was pleased to hear it, and would have continued his speech, but his breath suddenly went from him, and the unfinished curse died out in a gasp. Gunner Barnabas had put up one of his huge feet. "There's just enough room now for you to breathe, Shacklock," said he, "an' not enough for you to try to interrupt the conversashin I'm a-havin' with this gentleman. Choop!" Turning to me. Gunner Barnabas pulled at his pipe, but showed no hurry to open the "conversashin." I felt embarrassed, for, after all, the thus strangely unearthed difference between the Gunner and the Line man was no affair of mine. "Don't you go," said Gunner Barnabas. He had evidently been deeply moved by something. He dropped his head between his fists and looked steadily at me.

"I met this child 'ere," said he, "at Deelally—a fish-back recruity as ever was. I knowed 'im at Deelally, and I give 'im a latherin' at Deelally all for to keep 'im straight, 'e bein' such as wants a latherin' an' knowin' nuthin' o' the ways o' this country. Then I meets 'im up here, a butterfly-huntin' as innercent as you please—convalessin'. I goes out with 'im butterfly-huntin', and, as you see 'ere, a-shootin'. The gun betwixt us." I saw then, what I had overlooked before, a Company fowling-piece lying among some boulders far down the hill. Gunner Barnabas continued: "I should ha' seen where he had a-bin to get that drink inside o' 'im. Presently, 'e misses summat. 'You're a bloomin' fool,' sez I. 'If that had been a Pathan, now!' I sez. 'Damn yoiu' Pathans, an' you, too,' sez 'e. 'I strook it.' 'You did not,' I sez, 'I saw the bark fly.' 'Stick to your bloomin' pop-guns,' sez 'e, 'an' don't talk to a better man than you.' I laughed there, knowin' what I was an' what 'e was. 'You laugh?' sez he. 'I laugh' I sez, 'Shaddock, an' for what should I not laugh?' sez I. 'Then go an' laugh in Hell' sez 'e, 'for I'll 'ave none of your laughin'' With that 'e brings up the gun yonder and looses off, and I stretches 'im there, and guv him a little to keep 'im quiet, and puts 'im under, an' while I was thinkin' what nex', you comes down the 'ill, an' finds us as we was."

The Private was the Gunner's prey—I knew that the affair had fallen as the Gunner had said, for my friend is constitutionally incapable of lying—and I recognised that in his hands lay the boy's fate.

"What do you think?" said Gunner Barnabas, after a silence broken only by the convulsive breathing of the boy he was sitting on. "I think nothing," I said. "He didn't go at me. He's your property." Then an idea occurred to me. "Hand him over to his own Company. They'll school him half dead." "Got no Comp'ny," said Gimner Barnabas. "'E's a conv'lessint draft—all sixes an' sevens. Don't matter to them what he did." "Thrash him yourself, then," I said. Gunner Barnabas looked at the man and smiled; then caught up an arm, as a mother takes up the dimpled arm of a child, and ran the sleeve and shirt up to the elbow. "Look at that!" he said. It was a pitiful arm, lean and muscleless. "Can you mill a man with an arm like that—such as I would like to mill him, an' such as he deserves? I tell you, sir, an' I am not smokin' (swaggering), as you see—I could take that man—Sodger 'e is, Lord 'elp 'im!—an' twis' off 'is arms an' 'is legs as if 'e was a naked crab. See here!"

Before I could realise what was going to happen, Gimner Barnabas rose up, stooped, and takmg the wretched Private Shacklock by two points of grasp, heaved him up above his head. The boy kicked once or twice, and then was still. He was very white. "I could now," said Gunner Barnabas, "I could now chuck this man where I like. Chuck him like a lump o' beef, an' it would not be too much for him if I chucked. Can I thrash such a man with both 'ands? No, nor yet with my right 'and tied behind my back, an' my lef' in a sling,"

He dropped Private Shaddock on the ground and sat upon him as before. The boy groaned as the weight settled, but there was a look in his white-lashed, red eyes that was not pleasant.

"I do not know what I will do," said Gunner Barnabas, rocking himself to and fro. "I know 'is breed, an' the way o' the likes o' them. If I was in 'is Comp'ny, an' this 'ad 'appened, an' I 'ad struck 'im, as I would ha' struck him, 'twould ha' all passed off an' bin forgot till the drink was in 'im again—a month, maybe, or six, maybe. An' when the drink was frizzin' in 'is 'ead he would up and loose off in the night or the day or the evenin'. All acause of that millin' that 'e would ha' forgotten in betweens. That I would be dead— killed by the likes o' 'im, an' me the next strongest man but three in the British Army!"

Private Shacklock, not so hardly pressed as he had been, found breath to say that if he could only get hold of the fowling-piece again the strongest man but three in the British Army would be seriously crippled for the rest of his days. "Hear that!" said Gunner Barnabas, sitting heavily to silence his chair. "Hear that, you that think things is funny to put into the papers! He would shoot me, 'e would, now; an' so long as he's drunk, or comin' out o' the drink, 'e will want to shoot me. Look a-here!"

He turned the boy's head sideways, his hand round the nape of the neck, his thumb touching the angle of the jaw. "What do you call those marks?" They were the white scars of scrofula, with which Shacklock was eaten up. I told Gunner Barnabas this. "I don't know what that means. I call 'em murder-marks an' signs. If a man 'as these things on 'im, an' drinks, so long as 'e's drunk, 'e's mad—a looney. But that doesn't 'elp if 'e kills you. Look a-here, an' here!" The marks were thick on the jaw and neck. "Stubbs 'ad 'em," said Gunner Barnabas to himself, "an' Lancy 'ad 'em, an' Duggard 'ad 'em, an' wot's come to them? You've got 'em," he said, addressing himself to the man he was handling like a roped calf, "an' sooner or later you'll go with the rest of 'em. But this time I will not do anything—exceptin' keep you here till the drink's dead in you."

Gunner Barnabas resettled himself and continued: "Twice this afternoon, Shaddock, you 'ave been so near dyin' that I know no man more so. Once was when I stretched you, an' might ha' wiped off your face with my boot as you was lyin'; an' once was when I lifted you up in my fists. Was you afraid, Shacklock?"

"I were," murmured the half-stifled soldier.

"An' once more I will show you how near you can go to Kingdom Come in my 'ands." He knelt by Shaddock's side, the boy lying still as death. "If I was to hit you here," said he, "I would break your chest, an' you would die. If I was to put my 'and here, an' my other 'and here, I would twis' your neck, an' you would die, Privite Shacklock. If I was to put my knees here an' put your 'ead so, I would pull off your 'ead, Privite Shacklock, an' you would die. If you think as how I am a liar, say so, an' I'll show you. Do you think so?"

"No," whispered Private Shacklock, not daring to move a muscle, for Bamabas's hand was on his neck.

"Now, remember," went on Barnabas, "neither you will say nothing nor I will say nothing o' what has happened. I ha' put you to shame before me an' this gentleman here, an' that is enough. But I tell you, an' you give 'eed now, it would be better for you to desert than to go on a-servin' where you are now. If I meets you again—if my Batt'ry lays with your Reg'ment, an' Privite Shacklock is on the rolls, I will first mill you myself till you can't see, and then I will say why I strook you. You must go, an' look bloomin' slippy about it, for if you stay, so sure as God made Paythans an' we've got to wipe 'em out, you'll be loosing off o' unauthorised amminition—in or out o' barricks, an' you'll be 'anged for it. I know your breed, an' I know what these 'ere white marks mean. You're mad, Shacklock, that's all—and here you stay, under me. An' now choop, an' lie still."

I waited and smoked, and Gimner Barnabas smoked till the shadows lengthened on the hillside, and a chilly wind began to blow. At dusk Gunner Barnabas rose and looked at his captive. "Drink's out o' 'im now," he said.

"I can't move," whimpered Shacklock. "I've got the fever back again."

"I'll carry you," said Gunner Barnabas, swinging hun up and preparing to climb the hill. "Good-night, sir," he said to me. "It looks pretty, doesn't it? But never you forget, an' I won't forget neither, that this 'ere shiverin', shakin', convalescent a-hangin' on to my neck is a ragin', tearin' devil when 'e's lushy—an' 'e a boy!"

He strode up to the hill with his burden, but just before he disappeared he turned round and shouted: "It's the likes o' 'im brings shame on the likes o' us. 'Tain't we ourselves, s'elp me Gawd, 'tain't!"

His Brother's Keeper

"Whist?"

"Can't make up a four?"

"Poker, then?"

"Never again with you, Robin. 'Tisn't good enough, old man."

"Seeking what he may devour," murmured a third voice from behind a newspaper. "Stop the punkah, and make him go away."

"Don't talk of it on a night like this. It's enough to give a man fits. You've no enterprise. Here I've taken the trouble to come over after dinner—"

"On the off-chance of skinning some one. I don't believe you ever crossed a horse for pleasure."

"That's true, I never did—and there are only two Johnnies in the Club."

"They've all gone off to the Gaff."

"Wah! Wah! They must be pretty hard up for amusement. Help me to a split."

"Split in this weather! Hi, bearer, do burra—burra whiskey-peg lao, and just put all the barf into them that you can find."

The newspaper came down with a rustle, as the reader said:

"How the deuce d'you expect a man to improve his mind when you two are bukking about drinks? Qui hai! Mera wasti bhi."

"Oh! you're alive, are you? I thought pegs would fetch you out of that. Game for a little poker?"

"Poker—poker—red-hot poker! Saveloy, you're too generous. Can't you let a man die in peace?"

"Who's going to die?"

"I am, please the pigs, if it gets much hotter and that bearer doesn't bring the peg quickly."

"All right. Die away, mon ami. Only don't do it in the Club, that's all. Can't have it littered up with dead members. Houligan would object."

"By Jove! I think I can imagine old Houligan doing it. 'Member dead in the ante-room? Good Gud! Bless my soul! Impossible to run a Club this way. Call the Babu and see if his last month's bill is paid. Not paid! Good Gud! Bless my soul! Impossible to run a Club this way. Babu, attach that body till the bill is paid.' Revel, you might just hurry up your dying once in a way to give us the pleasure of seeing Houligan perform."

"I'll die legitimately," said Revel. "I'm not going to create a fresh scandal in the station. I'll wait for heat-apoplexy, or whatever is going, to come and fetch me."

"This is pukka hot-weather talk," said Saveloy. "I come over for a little honest poker, and find two moderately sensible men, Revel and Dallston, talking tombs. I'm sorry I've thrown away my valuable evening."

"D'you expect us to talk about buttercups and daisies, then?" said Dallston.

"No, but there's some sort of medium between those and Sudden Death."

"There isn't. I haven't seen a daisy for seven years, and now I want to die," said Revel, plunging luxuriously into his peg.

"I knew a Johnnie on the Frontier once who did," began Dallston meditatively.

"Half a minute. Bearer, cherut lao! Tobacco soothes the nerves when a man is expecting to hear a whacker. We know what your Frontier stories are, Martha."

Dallston had once, in a misguided moment, taken the part of Martha in the burlesque of Faust, and the nickname stuck.

"'Tisn't a whacker, it's a fact. He told me so himself."

"They always do, Martha. I've noticed that before. But what did he tell you?"

"He told me that he had died."

"Was that all? Explain him."

"It was this way. The man went down with a bad go of fever and was off his head. About the second day it struck him in the middle of the night."

"Steady the Buffs! Martha, you aren't an Irishman yet."

"Never mind. It's too hot to put it correctly. In the middle of the night he woke up quite calm, and it struck him that it would be a good thing to die—just as it might ha' struck him that it would be a good thing to put ice on his head. He lay on his bed and thought it over, and the more he thought about it, the better sort of bundobust it seemed to be. He was quite calm, you know, and he said that he could have sworn that he had no fever on him."

"Well, what happened?"

"Oh, he got up and loaded his revolver—he remembers all this—and let fly, with the muzzle to his temple. The thing didn't go off, so he turned it up and found he'd forgot to load one chamber."

"Better stop the tale there. We can guess what's coming."

"Hang it! It's a true yam. Well, he jammed the thing to his head again, and it missed fire, and he said that he felt ready to cry with rage, he was so disgusted. So he took it by the muzzle and hit himself on the head with it."

"Good man! Didn't it go off then?"

"No, but the blow knocked him silly, and he thought he was dead. He was awfully pleased, for he had been fiddling over the show for nearly half an hour. He dropped down and died. When he got his wits again, he was shaking with the fever worse than ever, but he had sense enough to go and knock up the doctor and give himself into his charge as a lunatic. Then he went clean off his head till the fever wore out."

"That's a good story," said Revel critically. "I didn't think you had it in you at this season of the year."

"I can believe it," said the man they called Saveloy. "Fever makes one do all sorts of queer things. I suppose your friend was mad with it when he discovered it would be so healthy to die."

"S'pose so. The fever must have been so bad that he felt all right—same way that a man who is nearly mad with drink gets to look sober. Well, anyhow, there was a man who died."

"Did he tell you what it felt like?"

"He said that he was awfully happy until his fever came back and shook him up. Then he was sick with fear. I don't wonder. He'd had rather a narrow escape."

"That's nothing," said Saveloy. "I know a man who lived."

"So do I," said Revel. "Lots of 'em, confound 'em."

"Now, this takes Martha's story, and it's quite true."

"They always are," said Martha. "I've noticed that before."

"Never mind, I'll forgive you. But this happened to me. Since you are talking tombs, I'll assist at the seance. It was in '82 or '88, I have forgotten which. Anyhow, it was when I was on the Utamamula Canal Headworks, and I was chumming with a man called Stovey. You've never met him because he belongs to the Bombay side, and if he isn't really dead by this he ought to be somewhere there now. He was a pukka sweep, and I hated him. We divided the Canal bimgalow between us, and we kept strictly to our own side of the buildings."

"Hold on! I call. What was Stovey to look at?" said Revel.

"Living picture of the King of Spades—a blackish, greasy sort of ruffian who hadn't any pretence of manners or form. He used to dine in the kit he had been messing about the Canal in all day, and I don't believe he ever washed. He had the embankments to look after, and I was in charge of the headworks, but he was always contriving to fall foul of me if he possibly could."

"I know that sort of man. Mullane of Ghoridasah's built that way."

"Don't know Mullane, but Stovey was a sweep. Canal work isn't exactly cheering, and it doesn't take you into much society. We were like a couple of rats in a burrow, grubbing and scooping all day and turning in at night into the barn of a bungalow. Well, this man Stovey didn't get fever. He was so coated with dirt that I don't believe the fever could have got at him. He just began to go mad."

"Cheerful! What were the symptoms?"

"Well, his naturally vile temper grew infamous. It was really unsafe to speak to him, and he always seemed anxious to murder a coolie or two. With me, of course, he restrained himself a little, but he sulked like a bear for days and days together. As he was the only European society within sixty miles, you can imagine how nice it was for me. He'd sit at table and sulk and stare at the opposite wall by the hour—instead of doing his work. When I pointed out that the Government didn't send us into these cheerful places to twiddle our thimibs, he glared like a beast. Oh, he was a thorough hog! He had a lot of other endearing tricks, but the worst was when he began to pray."

"Began to—how much?"

"Pray. He'd got hold of an old copy of the War Cry and used to read it at meals; and I suppose that that, on the top of tough goat, disordered his intellect. One night I heard him in his room groaning and talking at a fearful rate. Next morning I asked him if he'd been taken worse. 'I've been engaged in prayer,' he said, looking as black as thunder. 'A man's spiritual concerns are his own property.' One night—he'd kept up these spiritual exercises for about ten days, growing queerer and queerer every day—he said ' Good-night' after dinner, and got up and shook hands with me."

"Bad sign, that," said Revel, sucking industriously at his cheroot.

"At first I couldn't make out what the man wanted. No fellow shakes hands with a fellow he's living with—least of all such a beast as Stovey. However, I was civil, but the minute after he'd left the room it struck me what he was going to do. If he hadn't shaken hands I'd have taken no notice, I suppose. This unusual effusion put me on my guard."

"Curious thing! You can nearly always tell when a Johnnie means pegging out. He gives himself away by some softening. It's human nature. What did you do?"

"Called him back, and asked him what the this and that he meant by interfering with my coolies in the day. He was generally hampering my men, but I had never taken any notice of his vagaries till then. In another minute we were arguing away, hammer and tongs. If it had been any other man I'd 'a' simply thrown the lamp at his head. He was calling me all the mean names under the sum, accusing me of misusing my authority and goodness only knows what all. When he had talked himself down one stretch, I had only to say a few words to start him off again, as fresh as a daisy. On my word, this jabbering went on for nearly three hours."

"Why didn't you get coolies and have him tied up, if you thought he was mad?" asked Revel.

"Not a safe business, believe me. Wrongful restraint on your own responsibility of a man nearly your own standing looks ugly. Well, Stovey went on bullying me and complaining about everything I'd ever said or done since I came on the Canal, till—he went fast asleep."

"Wha-at?"

"Went off dead asleep, just as if he'd been drugged. I thought the brute had had a fit at first, but there he was, with his head hanging a little on one side and his mouth open. I knocked up his bearer and told him to take the man to bed. We carried him off and shoved him on his charpoy. He was still asleep, and I didn't think it worth while to undress him. The fit, whatever it was, had worked itself out, and he was limp and used up. But as I was going to leave the room, and went to turn the lamp down, I looked in the glass and saw that he was watching me between his eyelids. When I spun round he seemed asleep. 'That's your game, is it?' I thought, and I stood over him long enough to see that he was shamming. Then I cast an eye round the room and saw his Martini in the comer. We were all bullumteers on the Canal works. I couldn't find the cartridges, so to make all serene I knocked the breech-pin out with the cleaning-rod and went to my own room. I didn't go to sleep for some time. About one o'clock—our rooms were only divided by a door of sorts, and my bed was close to it—I heard my friend open a chest of drawers. Then he went for the Martini. Of course, the breechblock came out with a rattle. Then he went back to bed again, and I nearly laughed.

"Next morning he was doing the genial, hail-fellow-well-met trick. Said he was afraid he'd lost his temper overnight, and apologised for it. About half way through breakfast—he was talking thickly about everything and anything—he said he'd come to the conclusion that a beard was a beastly nuisance and made one stuffy. He was going to shave his. Would I lend him my razors? 'Oh, you're a crafty beast, you are,' I said to myself. I told him that I was of the other opinion, and finding my razors nearly worn out had chucked them into the Canal only the night before. He gave me one look under his eyebrows and went on with his breakfast. I was in a stew lest the man should cut his throat with one of the breakfast knives, so I kept one eye on him most of the time.

"Before I left the bungalow I caught old Jeewun Singh, one of the mistries on the gates, and gave him strict orders that he was to keep in sight of the Sahib wherever he went and whatever he did; and if he did or tried to do anything foolish, such as jumping down the well, Jeewim Singh was to stop him. The old man tumbled at once, and I was easier in my mind when I saw how he was shadowing Stovey up and down the works. Then I sat down and wrote a letter to old Baggs, the Civil Surgeon at Chemanghath, about sixty miles off, telling him how we stood. The runner left about three o'clock. Jeewun Singh turned up at the end of the day and gave a full, true and particular account of Stovey's doings. D'you know what the brute had done?"

"Spare us the agony. Kill him straight off, Saveloy!"

"He'd stopped the runner, opened the bag, read my letter and torn it up! There were only two letters in the bag, both of which I'd written. I was pretty average angry, but I lay low. At dinner he said he'd got a touch of dysentery and wanted some chlorodyne. For a man anxious to depart this life he was about as badly equipped as you could wish. Hadn't even a medicine-chest to play with. He was no more suffering from dysentery than I, but I said I'd give him the chlorodyne, and so I did—fifteen drops, mixed in a wine-glass, and when he asked for the bottle I said that I hadn't any more.

"That night he began praying again, and I just lay in bed and shuddered. He was invoking the most blasphemous curses on my head—all in a whisper, for fear of waking me up—for frustrating what he called his 'great and holy purpose.' You never heard anything like it. But as long as he was praying I knew he was alive, and he ran his praying half through the night.

"Well, for the next ten days he was apparently quite rational; but I watched him and told Jeewun Singh to watch him like a cat. I suppose he wanted to throw me off my guard, but I wasn't to be thrown. I grew thin watching him. Baggs wrote in to say he had gone on tour and couldn't be found anywhere in paiticular for another six weeks. It was a ghastly time.

"One day& old Jeewun Singh turned up with a bit of paper that Storey had given to one of the lohars as a naksha. I thought it was mean work spying into another man's very plans, but when I saw what was on the paper I gave old Jeewun Singh a rupee. It was a be-autiful little breech-pin. The one-idead idiot had gone back to Martini! I never dreamt of such persistence. 'Tell me when the lohar gives it to the Sahib,' I said, and I felt more comfy for a few days. Even if Jeewun Singh hadn't split I would have known when the new breechpin was made. The brute came in to dinner with a dashed confident, triumphant air, as if he'd done me in the eye at last; and all through dinner he was fiddling in his waistcoat pocket. He went to bed early. I went, too, and I put my head against the door and listened like a woman. I must have been shivering in my pyjamas for about two hours before my friend went for the dismantled Martin! He could not get the breech-pin to fit at first. He rummaged about, and then I heard a file go. That seemed to make too much noise to suit his fancy, so he opened the door and went out into the compound, and I heard him, about fifty yards off, filing in the dark at that breech-pin as if he had been possessed. Well, he was you know. Then he came back to the light, cursing me for keeping him out of his rest and the peace of Abraham's bosom. As soon as I heard him taking up the Martini, I ran round to his door and tried to enter gaily, as the stage directions say. 'Lend me your gun, old man, if you're awake,' I said. 'There's a howling big brute of a pariah in my room, and I want to get a shot at it.' I pretended not to notice that he was standing over the gun, but just pranced up and caught hold of it. He turned round with a jump and said: 'I'm sick of this. I'll see that dog, and if it's another of your lies I'll—' You know I'm not a moral man.'"

"Hear! Hear!" drowsily from Martha.

"But I simply daren't repeat what he said. 'All right!' I said, still hanging on to the gun.

'Come along and we'll bowl him over.' He followed me into my room with a face like a fiend in torment And, as truly as I'm yarning here, there was a huge brindled beast of a pariah sitting on my bed!"

"Tall, sir, tall. But go on. The audience is now awake."

"Hang it! Could I have invented that pariah? Stovey dropped of the gun and flopped down in a comer and yowled. I went 'ee ki ri ki re!' like a woman in hysterics, pitched the gun forward and loosed off through a window."

"And the pariah?"

"He quitted for the time being. Stovey was in an awful state. He swore the animal hadn't been there when I called him. That was true enough. I firmly believe Providence put it there to save me from being killed by the infuriated Stovey."

"You've too lively a belief in Providence altogether. What happened?"

"Stovey tried to recover himself and pass it all over, but he let me keep the gun and went to bed. About two days afterwards old Baggs turned up on tour, and I told him Stovey wanted watching—more than I could give him. I don't know whether Baggs or the pi did it, but he didn't throw any more suicidal splints. I was transferred a little while afterwards."

"Ever meet the man again?"

"Yes; once at Sheik Katan dâk bungalow—trailing the big brindle pi after him."

"Oh, it was real, then. I thought it was arranged for the occasion."

"Not a bit. It was a pukka pi. Stovey seemed to remember me in the same way that a horse seems to remember. I fancy his brain was a little cloudy. We tiffined together—after the pi had been fed, if you please—and Stovey said to me: 'See that dog? He saved my life once. Oh, by the way, I believe you were there, too, weren't you?' I shouldn't care to work with Stovey again."

There was a holy pause in the smoking-room of the Toopare Club.

"What I like about Saveloy's play," said Martha, looking at the ceiling, "is the beautifully artistic way in which he follows up a flush with a full. Go to bed, old man!'

"Sleipner," Late "Thurinda"

There are men, both good and wise, who hold that in a future state
Dumb creatures we have cherished here below

Will give us joyous welcome as we pass the Golden Gate.
Is it folly if I hope it may be so?
—The Place Where the Old Horse Died.

If there were any explanation available here, I should be the first person to offer it. Unfortunately, there is not, and I am compelled to confine myself to the facts of the case as vouched for by Hordene and confirmed by "Guj," who is the last man in the world to throw away a valuable horse for nothing.

Jale came up with Thurinda to the Shayid Spring meeting; and besides Thurinda his string included Divorce, Meg's Diversions and Benoni—ponies of sorts. He won the Officers' Scurry—five furlongs—with Benoni on the first day, and that sent up the price of the stable in the evening lotteries; for Benoni was the worst-looking of the three, being a pigeontoed, split-chested dâk horse, with a wonderful gift of blundering in on his shoulders—ridden out to the last ounce—but first. Next day Jale was riding Divorce in the Wattle and Dab Stakes—around the jump course; and she turned over at the on-and-off course when she was leading and managed to break her neck. She never stirred from the place where she dropped, and Jale did not move either till he was carried off the ground to his tent close to the big shamiana where the lotteries were held. He had ricked his back, and everything below the hips was as dead as timber. Otherwise he was perfectly well. The doctor said that the stiffness would spread and that he would die before the next morning. Jale insisted upon knowing the worst, and when he heard it sent a pencil note to the Honorary Secretary, saying that they were not to stop the races or do anything foolish of that kind. If he hung on till the next day the nominations for the third day's racing would not be void, and he would settle up all claims before he threw up his hand. This relieved the Honorary Secretary, because most of the horses had come from a long distance, and, under any circumstance, even had the Judge dropped dead in the box, it would have been impossible to have postponed the racing. There was a great deal of money on the third day, and five or six of the owners were gentlemen who would make even one day's delay an excuse. Well, settling would not be easy. No one knew much about Jale. He was an outsider from down country, but every one hoped that, since he was doomed, he would live through the third day and save trouble.

Jale lay on his charpoy in the tent and asked the doctor and the man who catered to the refreshments— he was the nearest at the time—to witness his will. "I don't know how long my arms will be workable," said Jale, "and we'd better get this business over." The private arrangements of the will concern nobody but Jale's friends; but there was one clause that was rather curious. "Who was that man with the brindled hair who put me up for a night util the tent was ready? The man who rode down to pick me up when I was smashed. Nice sort of fellow he seemed." "Hordene?" said the doctor. "Yes, Hordene. Good chap, Hordene. He keeps Bull whisky. Write down that I give this Johnnie Hordene Thurinda for his own, if he can sell the other ponies. Thurinda's a good mare. He can enter her—post-entry—for the All Horse Sweep if he likes—on the last day. Have you got that down? I suppose the Stewards'll recognise the gift?" "No trouble about that," said the doctor. "All right. Give him the other two ponies to sell. They're entered for the last day, but I shall be dead then. Tell him to send the money to—" Here he gave an address. "Now I'll sign and you sign, and that's all. This deadness is coming up between my shoulders."

Jale lived, dying very slowly, till the third day's racing, and up till the time of the lotteries on the fourth day's racing. The doctor was rather surprised. Hordene came in to thank him for his gift, and to suggest it would be much better to sell Thurinda with the others. She was the best of them all, and would have fetched twelve hundred on her looking-over merits only. "Don't you bother," said Jale. "You take her. I rather liked you. I've got no people, and that Bull whisky was firstclass stuff. I'm pegging out now, I think."

The lottery-tent outside was beginning to fill, and Jale heard the click of the dice. "That's all right," said he. "I wish I was there, but—I'm—going to the drawer." Then he died quietly. Hordene went into the lottery-tent, after calling the doctor. "How's Jale?" said the Honorary Secretary. "Gone to the drawer," said Hordene, settling into a chair and reaching out for a lottery paper, "Poor beggar!" said the Honorary Secretary. "'Twasn't the fault of our on-and-off, though. The mare blundered. Gentlemen! gentlemen! Nine hundred and eighty rupees in the lottery, and River of Years for sale!" The lottery lasted far into the night, and there was a supplementary lottery on the All Horse Sweep, where Thurinda sold for a song, and was not bought by her owner. , "It's not lucky," said Hordene, and the rest of the men agreed with him. "I ride her myself, but I don't know anything about her and I wish to goodness I hadn't taken her," said he. "Oh, bosh I Never refuse a horse or a drink, however you come by them. No one objects, do they? Not going to refer this matter to Calcutta, are we? Here, somebody, bid! Eleven hundred and fifty rupees in the lottery, and Thurinda—absolutely imknown, acquired under the most romantic circumstances from about the toughest man it has ever been my good fortune to meet—for sale. Hullo, Nurji, is that you? Gentlemen, where a Pagan bids shall enlightened Christians hang back? Ten! Going, going, gone!" "You want ha-af, sar?" said the battered native trainer to Hordene. "No, thanks—not a bit of her for me."

The All Horse Sweep was run, and won by Thurinda by about a street and three-quarters, to be very accurate, amid derisive cheers, which Hordene, who flattered himself that he knew something about riding, could not uderstand. On pulling up he looked over his shoulder and saw that the second horse was only just passing the box. "Now, how did I make such a fool of myself?" he said as he returned to weigh out. His friends gathered round him and asked tenderly whether this was the first time that he had got up, and whether it was absolutely necessary that the winning horse should be ridden out when the field were hopelessly pumped, a quarter of a mile behind, etc., etc. "I—I—thought River of Years was pressing me," explained Hordene. "River of Years was wallowing, absolutely wallowing," said a man, "before you turned into the straight. You rode like a—hang it—like a Militia subaltern!"

The Shayid Spring meeting broke up and the sportsmen turned their steps towards the next carcase— the Ghoriah Spring. With them went Thurinda's owner, the happy possessor of an almost perfect animal. "'She's as easy as a Pullman car and about twice as fast," he was wont to say in moments of confidence to his intimates. "For all her bulk, she's as handy as a polo-pony; a child might ride her, and when she's at the post she's as cute—she's as cute as the bally starter himself." Many times had Hordene said this, till at last one imsympathetic friend answered with: "When a man bukhs too much about his wife or his horse, it's a sure sign he's trying to make himself like 'em. I mistrust your Thurinda. She's too good, or else—" "Or else what?" "You're trying to believe you like her." "Like her! I love her! I trust that darling as I'm shot if I'd trust you. I'd hack her for tuppence." "Hack away, then. I don't want to hurt your feelings. I don't hack my stable myself, but some horses go better for it. Come and peacock at the band-stand this evening." To the band-stand accordingly Hordene came, and the lovely Thurinda comported herself with all the gravity and decorum that might have been expected. Hordene rode home with the scoffer, through the dusk, discoursing on matters indifferent. "Hold up a minute," said his friend, "there's Gagley riding behind us." Then, raising his voice: "Come along, Gagley! I want to speak to you about the Race Ball." But no Gagley came; and the couple went forward at a trot. "Hang it! There's that man behind us still." Hordene listened and could clearly hear the sound of a horse trotting, apparently just behind them. "Come on, Gagley! Don't play bo-peep in that ridiculous way," shouted the friend. Again no Gagley. Twenty yards farther there was a crash and a stumble as the friend's horse came down over an unseen rat-hole. "How much damaged?" asked Hordene. "Sprained my wrist," was the dolorous answer, "and there is something wrong with my knee-cap. There' goes my mount to-morrow, and this gee is cut like a cab-horse."

On the first day of the Ghoriah meeting Thurinda was hopelessly ridden out by a native jockey, to whose care Hordene had at the last moment been compelled to confide her. "You forsaken idiot!" said he, "what made you begin riding as soon as you were clear? She had everything safe, if you'd only left her alone. You rode her out before the home turn, you hog!" "What could I do?" said the jockey sullenly. "I was pressed by another horse." "Whose 'other horse'? There were twenty yards of daylight between you and the ruck. If you'd kept her there even then 'twouldn't ha' mattered. But you rode her out—you rode her out!" "There was another horse and he pressed me to the end, and when I looked round he was no longer there." Let us, in charity, draw a veil over Hordene's language at this point. "Goodness knows whether she'll be fit to pull out again for the last event. D—n you and your other horses! I wish I'd broken your neck before letting you get up!" Thurinda was done to a turn, and it seemed a cruelty to ask her to run again in the last race of the day. Hordene rode this time, and was careful to keep the mare within herself at the outset. Once more Thurinda left her field—with one exception—a grey horse that hung upon her flanks and could not be shaken off. The mare was done, and refused to answer the call upon her. She tried hopelessly in the straight and was caught and passed by her old enemy, River of Years—the chestnut of Kumaul. "You rode well—like a native, Hordene," was the unflattering comment, "The mare was ridden out before River of Years," "But the grey," began Hordene, and then ceased, for he knew that there was no grey in the race. Blue Point and Diamond Dust, the only greys at the meeting, were running in the Arab Handicap.

He caught his native jockey. "What horse, d'you say, pressed you?" "I don't know. It was a grey with nutmeg tickings behind the saddle." That evening Hordene sought the great Major Blare-Tyndar, who knew personally the father, mother and ancestors of almost every horse, brought from ekka or ship, that had ever set foot on an Indian race-course. "Say, Major, what is a grey horse with nutmeg tickings behind the saddle?" "A curiosity. Wendell Holmes is a grey, with nutmeg on the near shoulder, but there is no horse marked your way, now. Then, after a pause: "No, I'm wrong—you ought to know. The pony that got you Thurinda was grey and nutmeg." "How much?" "Divorce, of course. The mare that broke her neck at the Shayid meeting and killed Jale. A big thirteen-three she was. I recollect when she was hacking old Snuffy Beans to office. He bought her from a dealer, who had her left on his hands as a rejection when the Pink Hussars were buying team up country and then—Hullo! The man's gone!" Hordene had departed on receipt of information which he already knew. He only demanded extra confirmation. Then he began to argue with himself, bearing in mind that he himself was a sane man, neither gluttonous nor a wine-bibber, with an unimpaired digestion, and that Thurinda was to all appearance a horse of ordinary flesh and exceedingly good blood. Arrived at these satisfactory conclusions, he reargued the whole matter.

Being by nature intensely superstitious, he decided upon scratching Thurinda and facing the howl of indignation that would follow. He also decided to leave the Ghoriah meet and change his luck. But it would have been sinful—positively wicked—to have left without waiting for the polo-match that was to conclude the festivities. At the last moment before the match, one of the leading players of the Ghoriah team and Hordene's host discovered that, through the kindly foresight of his head sais, every single pony had been taken down to the ground. "Lend me a hack, old man," he shouted to Hordene as he was changing. "Take Thurinda" was the reply. "She'll bring you down in ten minutes.'" And Thurinda was accordingly saddled for Marish's benefit. "I'll go down with you," said Hordene. The two rode off together at a hand canter. "By Jove! Somebody's sais 'll get kicked for this!" said Marish, looking round. "Look there! He's coming for the mare! Pull out into the middle of the road." "What on earth d'you mean?" "Well, if you can take a strayed horse so calmly, I can't. Didn't you see what a lather that grey was in?" "What grey?" "The grey that just passed us—saddle and all, He's got away from the ground, I suppose. Now he's turned the corner; but you can hear his hoofs. Listen!" There was a furious gallop of shod horses, gradually dying into silence. "Come along," said Hordene. "We're late as it is. We shall know all about it on the ground." "Anybody lost a tat?" asked Marish cheerily as they reached the ground. "No, we've lost you. Double up. You're late enough as it is. Get up and go in. The teams are waiting." Marish mounted his polo-pony and cantered across. Hordene watched the game idly for a few moments. There was a scrimmage, a cloud of dust, and a cessation of play, and a shouting for saises. The umpire clattered forward and returned. "What has happened?" "Marish! Neck broken! Nobody's fault. Pony crossed its legs and came down. Game's stopped. Thank God, he hasn't got a wife!" Again Hordene pondered as he sat on his horse's back. "Under any circumstances it was written that he was to be killed. I had no interest in his death, and he had his warning, I suppose. I can't make out the system that this infernal mare runs under. Why him? Anyway, I'll shoot her." He looked at Thurinda, the calm-eyed, the beautiful, and repented. "No! I'll sell her."

"What in the world has happened to Thurinda that Hordene is so keen on getting rid of her?" was the general question. "I want money," said Hordene unblushingly, and the few who knew how his accounts stood saw that this was a varnished lie. But they held their peace because of the great love and trust that exists among the ancient and honourable fraternity of sportsmen.

"There's nothing wrong with her," explained Hordene. "Try her as much as you like, but let her stay in my stable until you've made up your mind one way or the other. Nine hundred's my price."

"I'll take her at that," quoth a red-haired subaltern, nicknamed Carrots, later Gaja, and then, for brevity's sake, Guj. "Let me have her out this afternoon. I want her more for hacking than anything else."

Guj tried Thurinda exhaustively and had no fault to find with her. "She's all right," he said briefly. "I'll take her. It's a cash deal." "Virtuous Guj!" said Hordene, pocketing the cheque. "If you go on like this you'll be loved and respected by all who know you."

A week later Guj insisted that Hordene should accompany him on a ride. They cantered merrily for a time. Then said the subaltern: "Listen to the mare's beat a minute, will you? Seems to me that you've sold me two horses."

Behind the mare was plainly audible the cadence of a swiftly trotting horse. "D'you hear anything?" said Guj. "No—nothing but the regular triplet," said Hordene; and he lied when he answered. Guj looked at him keenly and said nothing. Two or three months passed and Hordene was perplexed to see his old property running, and running well. under the curious title of "Sldpner—late Thurinda." He consulted the Great Major, who said: "I don't know a horse called Sleipner, but I know of one. He was a northern bred, and belonged to Odin." "A mythologicalbeast?" "Exactly. Like Bucephalus and the rest of 'em. He was a great horse. I wish I had some of his get in my stable." "Why?" "Because he had eight legs. When he had used up one set, he let down the other four to come up the straight on. Stewards were lenient in those days. Now it's all you can do to get a crock with three sound legs."

Hordene cursed the red-haired Guj in his heart for finding out the mare's peculiarity. Then he cursed the dead man Jale for his ridiculous interference with a free gift. "If it was given—it was given," said Hordene, "and he has no right to come messing about after it." When Guj and he next met, he enquired tenderly after Thurinda. The red-haired subaltern, impassive as usual, answered: "I've shot her." "Well—you know your own affairs best," said Hordene. "You've given yourself away," said Guj. "What makes you think I shot a sound horse? She might have been bitten by a mad dog, or lamed." "You didn't say that." "No, I didn't, because I've a notion that you knew what was wrong with her." "Wrong with her! She was as sound as a bell—" "I know that. Don't pretend to misunderstand. You'll believe me, and I'll believe you in this show; but no one else will believe us. That mare was a bally nightmare." "Go on," said Hordene. "I stuck the noise of the other horse as long as I could, and called her Sleipner on the strength of it. Sleipner was a stallion, but that's a detail. When it got to interfering with every race I rode it was more than I could stick. I took her off racing, and, on my honour, since that time I've been nearly driven out of my mind by a grey and nutmeg pony. It used to trot round my quarters at night, fool about the Mall, and graze about the compound. You know that pony. It isn't a pony to catch or ride or hit, is it?" "No," said Hordene; "I've seen it." "So I shot Thurinda; that was a thousand rupees out of my pocket. And old Stiffer, who's got his new crematoriima in full blast, cremated her. I say, what was the matter with the mare? Was she bewitched?"

Hordene told the story of the gift, which Guj heard out to the end. "Now, that's a nice sort of yarn to tell in a messroom, isn't it? They'd call it junps or insanity," said Guj. "There's no reason in it. It doesn't lead up to anything. It only killed poor Marish and made you stick me with the mare; and yet it's true. Are you mad or drunk, or am I? That's the only explanation." "Can't be drunk for nine months on end, and madness would show in that time," said Hordene.

"All right," said Guj recklessly, going to the window. "I'll lay that ghost." He leaned out into the night and shouted: "Jale! Jale! Jale! Wherever you are." There was a pause and then up the compound-drive came the clatter of a horse's feet. The red-haired subaltern blanched under his freckles to the colour of glycerine soap. "Thurinda's dead," he muttered, "and—and all bets are off. Go back to your grave again."

Hordene was watching him open-mouthed.

"Now bring me a strait-jacket or a glass of brandy," said Guj. "That's enough to turn a man's hair white. What did the poor wretch mean by knocking about the earth?"

"Don't know," whispered Hordene hoarsely. "Let's get over to the Club. I'm feeling a bit shaky."

A Supplementary Chapter

Shall I not one day remember thy Bower—
One day when all days are one day to me?
Thinking I stirred not and yet had the power,
Yearning—ah, God, if again it might be!
—The Song of the Bower.

This is a base betrayal of confidence, but the sin is Mrs. Hauksbee's and not mine.

If you remember a certain foolish tale called "The Education of Otis Yeere," you will not forget that Mrs. Mallowe laughed at the wrong time, which was a single, and at Mrs. Hauksbee, which was a double, offence. An experiment had gone wrong, and it seems that Mrs. Mallowe had said some quaint things about the experimentrix.

"I am not angry," said Mrs. Hauksbee, "and I admire Polly in spite of her evil counsels to me. But I shall wait—I shall wait, like the frog footman in Alice in Wonderland, and Providence will deliver Polly into my hands. It always does if you wait." And she departed to vex the soul of the "Hawley boy," who says that she is singularly "uninstruite and childlike." He got that first word out of a Ouida novel. I do not know what it means, but am prepared to make an affidavit before the Collector that it does not mean Mrs. Hauksbee.

Mrs. Hauksbee's ideas of waiting are very liberal. She told the "Hawley boy" that he dared not tell Mrs. Reiver that "she was an intellectual woman with a gift for attracting men," and she offered another man two waltzes if he would repeat the same thing in the same ears. But he said: "Timeo Danaos et dona ferentes," which means "Mistrust all waltzes except those you get for legitimate asking."

The "Hawley boy" did as he was told because he believes in Mrs. Hauksbee. He was the instrument in the hand of a Higher Power, and he wore jharun coats, like "the scoriac rivers that roll their sulphurous torrents down Yahek, in the realms of the Boreal Pole," that made your temples throb when seen early in the morning. I will introduce him to you some day if all goes well. He is worth knowing.

Unpleasant things have already been written about Mrs. Reiver in other places.

She was a person without invention. She used to get her ideas from the men she captured, and this led to some eccentric changes of character. For a month or two she would act à la Madonna, and try Theo for a change if she fancied Theo's ways suited her beauty. Then she would attempt the dark and fiery Lilith, and so and so on, exactly as she had absorbed the new notion. But there was always Mrs. Reiver— hard, selfish, stupid Mrs. Reiver—at the back of each transformation. Mrs. Hauksbee christened her the Magic Lantern on account of this borrowed mutability. "It just depends upon the slide," said Mrs. Hauksbee. "The case is the only permanent thing in the exhibition. But that, thank Heaven, is getting old,"

There was a Fancy Ball at Government House and Mrs. Reiver came attired in some sort of '98 costume, with her hair pulled up to the top of her head, showing the clear outline on the back of the neck like the Récamier engravings. Mrs. Hauksbee had chosen to be loud, not to say vulgar, that evening, and went as The Black Death—a curious arrangement of barred velvet, black domino and flame-coloured satin puffery coming up to the neck and the wrists, with one of those shrieking keel-backed cicalas in the hair. The scream of the creature made people jump. It sounded so unearthly in a ballroom.

I heard her say to some one: "Let me introduce you to Madame Récamier," and I saw a man dressed as Autolycus bowing to Mrs. Reiver, while The Black Death looked more than usually saintly. It was a very pleasant evening, and Autolycus and Madame Recamier—I heard her ask Autolycus who Madame Récamier was, by the way—danced together ever so much. Mrs. Hauksbee was in a meditative mood, but she laughed once or twice in the back of her throat, and that meant trouble.

Autolycus was Trewinnard, the man whom Mrs. Mallowe had told Mrs. Hauksbee about—the Platonic Paragon, as Mrs. Hauksbee called him. He was amiable, but his moustache hid his mouth, and so he did not explain himself all at once. If you stared at him, he turned his eyes away, and through the rest of the dinner kept looking at you to see whether you were looking again. He took stares as a tribute to his merits, which were generally known and recognised. When he played billiards he apologised at length between each bad stroke, and explained what would have happened if the red had been somewhere else, or the bearer had trimmed the third lamp, or the wind hadn't made the door bang. Also he wriggled in his chair more than was becoming to one of his inches. Little men may wriggle and fidget without attracting notice. It doesn't suit big-framed men. He was the Main Girder Boom of the Kutcha, Pukka, Bimdobust and Benaoti Department and corresponded direct with the Three Taped Bashaw. Every one knows what that means. The men in his own office said that where anything was to be gained, even temporarily, he would never hesitate for a moment over handing up a subordinate to be hanged and drawn and quartered. He didn't back up his underlings, and for that reason they dreaded taking responsibility on their shoulders, and the strength of the Department was crippled.

A weak Department can, and often does, do a power of good work simply because its chief sees it through thick and thin. Mistakes may be born of this policy, but it is safe and sounder than giving orders which may be read in two ways and reserving to yourself the right of interpretation according to subsequent failure or success. Offices prefer administration to diplomacy. They are very like Empires.

Hatchett of the Almirah and Thannicutch—a vicious little three-cornered Department that was always stamping on the toes of the Elect—had the fairest estimate of Trewinnard, when he said: "I don't believe he is as good as he is." They always quoted that verdict as an instance of the blind jealousy of the Uncovenanted, but Hatchett was quite right. Trewinnard was just as good and no better than Mrs. Mallowe could make him; and she had been engaged on the work for three years. Hatchett has a narrow-minded partiality for the more than naked—the anatomised Truth—but he can gauge a man.

Trewinnard had been spoilt by over-much petting, and the devil of vanity that rides nine hundred and ninety-nine men out of a thousand made him behave as he did. He had been too long one woman's property; and that belief will sometimes drive a man to throw the best things in the world behind him, from rank perversity. Perhaps she only meant to stray temporarily and then return, but in arranging for this excursion he misimderstood both Mrs. Mallowe and Mrs. Reiver. The one made no sign, she would have died first; and the other—well, the high-falutin mindsome lay was her craze for the time being. She had never tried it before and several men had hinted that it would eminently become her. Trewinnard was in himself pleasant, with the great merit of belonging to somebody else. He was what they call "intellectual," and vain to the marrow. Mrs. Reiver returned his lead in the first, and hopelessly out-trumped him in the second suit. Put down all that comes after this to Providence or The Black Death.

Trewimiard never realised how far he had fallen from his allegiance till Mrs. Reiver referred to some official matter that he had been telling her about as "ours." He remembered then how that word had been sacred to Mrs. Mallowe and how she had asked his permission to use it. Opium is intoxicating, and so is whisky, but more intoxicating than either to a certain build of mind is the first occasion on which a woman—especially if she have asked leave for the "honour"—identifies herself with a man's work. The second time is not so pleasant. The answer has been given before, and the treachery comes to the top and tastes coppery in the mouth.

Trewinnard swallowed the shame—he felt dimly that he was not doing Mrs. Reiver any great wrong by untruth—and told and told and continued to tell, for the snare of this form of open-heartedness is that no man, unless he be a consummate liar, knows where to stop. The office door of all others must be either open wide or shut tight with a shaprassi to keep off callers.

Mrs. Mallowe made no sign to show that she felt Trewinnard's desertion till a piece of information that could only have come from one quarter ran about Simla like quicksilver. She met Trewinnard at a dinner. "Choose your confidantes better, Harold," she whispered as she passed him in the drawing-room. He turned salmon-colour, and swore very hard to himself that Babu Durga Charan Laha must go—must go—must go. He almost believed in that grey-headed old oyster's guilt.

And so another of those upside-down tragedies that we call a Simla Season wore through to the end—from the Birthday Ball to the "tripping" to Naldera and Kotghar. And fools gave feasts and wise men ate them, and they were bidden to the wedding and sat down to bake, and those who had nuts had no teeth and they staked the substance for the shadow, and carried coals to Newcastle, and in the dark all cats were grey, as it was in the days of the great Curé of Meudon.

Late in the year there developed itself a battle-royal between the K.P.B. and B. Department and the Almirah and Thannicutch. Three columns of this paper would be needed to supply you with the outlines of the difficulty; and then you would not be grateful. Hatchett snuffed the fray from afar and went into it with his teeth bared to the gums, while his Department stood behind him solid to a man. They believed in him, and their answer to the fury of men who detested him was: "Ah! But you'll admit he's damned right in what he says."

"The head of Trewinnard in a Government Resolution," said Hatchett, and he told the daftri to put a new pad on his blotter, and smiled a bleak smile as he spread out his notes. Hatchett is a Thug in his systematic way of butchering a man's reputation.

"What are you going to do?" asked Trewinnard's Department. "Sit tight," said Trewinnard, which was tantamount to saying "Lord knows." The Department groaned and said: "Which of us poor beggars is to be Jonahed this time?" They knew Trewinnard's vice.

The dispute was essentially not one for the K.P.B. and B. under its then direction to fight out. It should have been compromised, or at the worst sent up to the Supreme Government with a private and confidential note directing justice into the proper paths.

Some people say that the Supreme Government is the Devil. It is more like the Deep Sea. Anything that you throw into it disappears for weeks, and comes to light hacked and furred at the edges, crusted with weeds and shells and almost unrecognisable. The bold man who would dare to give it a file of love-letters would be amply rewarded. It would overlay them with original comments and marginal notes, and work them piecemeal into D. O. dockets. Few things, from a setter or a whirlpool to a sausage-machine or a hatching hen, are more interesting and peculiar than the Supreme Government.

"What shall we do?" said Trewinnard, who had fallen from grace into sin. "Fight," said Mrs. Reiver, or words to that effect; and no one can say how far aimless desire to test her powers, and how far belief in the man she had brought to her feet prompted the judgment. Of the merits of the case she knew just as much as any ayah.

Then Mrs. Mallowe, upon an evil word that went through Simla, put on her visiting-garb and attired herself for the sacrifice, and went to call—to call upon Mrs. Reiver, knowing what the torture would be. From half-past twelve till twenty-five minutes to two she sat, her hand upon her cardcase, and let Mrs. Reiver stab at her, all for the sake of the information. Mrs. Reiver double-acted her part, but she played into Mrs. Mallowe's hand by this defect. The assumptions of ownership, the little intentional slips, were overdone, and so also was the pretence of intimate knowledge. Mrs. Mallowe never winced. She repeated to herself: "And he has trusted this—this Thing. She knows nothing and she cares nothing, and she has digged this trap for him." The main feature of the case was abundantly clear. Trewinnard, whose capacities Mrs. Mallowe knew to the utmost farthing, to whom public and departmental petting were as the breath of his delicately-cut nostrils—Trewinnard, with his nervous dread of dispraise, was to be pitted against the Paul de Cassagnac of the Almirah and Thannicutch—the unspeakable Hatchett, who fought with the venom of a woman and the skill of a Red Indian. Unless his cause was triply just, Trewinnard was already under the guiotine. and if he had been under this "Thing's" dominance, small hope for the justice of his case. "Oh, why did I let him go without putting out a hand to fetch him back?" said Mrs. Mallowe, as she got into her 'rickshaw.

Now, Tim, her fox-terrier, is the only person who knows what Mrs. Mallowe did that afternoon, and as I found him loafing on the Mall in a very disconsolate condition and as he recognised me effusively and suggested going for a monkey-hunt—a thing he had never done before—my impression is that Mrs. Mallowe stayed at home till the light fell and thought. If she did this, it is of course hopeless to account for her actions. So you must fill in the gap for yourself.

That evening it rained heavily, and horses mired their riders. But not one of all the habits was so plastered with mud as the habit of Mrs. Mallowe when she pulled up under the scrub oaks and sent in her name by the astounded bearer to Trewinnard. "Folly! downright folly!" she said as she sat in the steam of the dripping horse. "But it's all a horrible jumble together."

It may be as well to mention that ladies do not usually call upon bachelors at their houses. Bachelors would scream and run away. Trewinnard came into the light of the verandah with a nervous, undecided smile upon his lips, and he wished—in the bottomless bottom of his bad heart—he wished that Mrs. Reiver was there to see. A minute later he was profoundly glad that he was alone, for Mrs. Mallowe was standing in his office room and calling him names that reflected no credit on his intellect. "What have you done? What have you said?' she asked. "Be quick! Be quick! And have the horse led round to the back. Can you speak? What have you written? Show me!"

She had interrupted him in the middle of what he was pleased to call his reply; for Hatchett's first shell had already fallen in the camp. He stood back and offered her the seat at the duftar table. Her elbow left a great wet stain on the baize, for she was soaked through and through.

"Say exactly how the matter stands," she said, and laughed a weak little laugh, which emboldened Trewinnard to say loftily: "Pardon me, Mrs. Mallowe, but I hardly recognise your—'

"Idiot! Will you show me the papers, will you speak, and will you be quick?"

Her most reverent admirers would hardly have recognised the soft-spoken, slow-gestured, quiet-eyed Mrs. Mallowe in the indignant woman who was drumming on Trewinnard's desk. He submitted to the voice of authority, as he had submitted in the old times, and explained as quickly as might be the cause of the war between the two Departments. In conclusion he handed over the rough sheets of his reply. As she read she watched her with the expectant sickly half-smile of the unaccustomed writer who is doubtful of the success of his work. And another smile followed, but died away as he saw Mrs. Mallowe read his production. All the old phrases out of which she had so carefully drilled him had returned; the unpruned fluency of diction was there, the more luxuriant for being so long cut back; the reckless riotousness of assertion that sacrificed all—even the vital truth that Hatchett would be so sure to take advantage of—for the sake of scoring a point, was there; and through and between every line ran the weak, wilful vanity of the man. Mrs. Mallowe's mouth hardened.

"And you wrote this!" she said. Then to herself: "He wrote this!"

Trewinnard stepped forward with a gesture habitual to him when he wished to explain. Mrs. Reiver had never asked for explanations. She had told him that all his ways were perfect. Therefore he loved her.

Mrs. Mallowe tore up the papers one by one, saying as she did so: "You were going to cross swords with Hatchett. Do you know your own strength? Oh, Harold, Harold, it is too pitiable! I thought—I thought—" Then the great anger that had been growing in her broke out, and she cried: "Oh, you fool! You blind, blind, blind, trumpery fool! Why do I help you? Why do I have anything to do with you? You miserable man! Sit down and write as I dictate. Quickly! And I had chosen you out of a hundred other men! Write! It is a terrible thing to be found out by a mere unseeing male—Thackeray has said it. It is worse, far worse, to be found out by a woman, and in that hour after long years to discover her worth. For ten minutes Trewinnard's pen scratched across the paper, and Mrs. Mallowe spoke. "And that is all," she said bitterly. "As you value yourself—your noble, honourable, modest self—keep within that."

But that was not all—by any means. At least as far as Trewinnard was concerned.

He rose from his chair and delivered his soul of many mad and futile thoughts—such things as a man babbles when he is deserted of the gods, has missed his hold upon the latch-door of Opportunity—and cannot see that the ways are shut. Mrs. Mallowe bore with him to the end, and he stood before her—no enviable creature to look upon.

"A cur as well as a fool!" she said. "Will you be good enough to tell them to bring my horse? I do not trust to your honour—you have none—but I believe that your sense of shame will keep you from speaking of my visit."

So he was left in the verandah crying "Come back" like a distracted guinea-fowl.

"He's done us in the eye," grunted Hatchett as he perused the K.P.B. and B. reply. "Look at the cunning of the brute in shifting the issue on to India in that carneying, blarneying way! Only wait until I can get my knife into him again. I'll stop every bolt-hole before the hunt begins."

Oh, I believe I have forgotten to mention the success of Mrs. Hauksbee's revenge. It was so brilliant and overwhelming that she had to cry in Mrs. Mallowe's arms for the better part of half an hour; and Mrs. Mallowe was just as bad, though she thanked Mrs. Hauksbee several times in the course of the interview, and Mrs. Hauksbee said that she would repent and reform, and Mrs. Mallowe said: "Hush, dear, hush! I don't think either of us had anything to be proud of." And Mrs. Hauksbee said: "Oh, but I didn't mean it, Polly, I didn't mean it!" And I stood with my hat in my hand trying to make two very indignant ladies imderstand that the bearer really had given me "salaam bolta."

That was an evil quarter minute.

Tells how the Professor and I found the Precious Rediculouses and how they Chautauquaed at us. Puts into print some sentiments better left unrecorded, and proves that a neglected theory will blossom in congenial soil. Contains fragments of three lectures and a confession.

"But these, in spite of careful dirt.
Are neither green nor sappy;
Half conscious of the garden squirt.
The Spendlings look unhappy,"

Out of the silence under the appletrees the Professor spake. One leg thrust from the hammock netting kicked lazily at the blue. There was the crisp crunch of teeth in an apple core.

"Get out of this," said the Professor lazily. As it was on the banks of the Hughli, so on the green borders of the Musquash and the Ohio—eternal unrest, and the insensate desire to go ahead. I was lapped in a very trance of peace. Even the apples brought no indigestion.

"Permanent Nuisance, what is the matter now?" I grunted.

"G'long out of this and go to Niagara," said the Professor in jerks. "Spread the ink of description through the waters of the Horseshoe falls—buy a papoose from the tame wild Indian who lives at the Clifton House—take a fifty-cent ride on the Maid of the Mist—go over the falls in a tub."

"Seriously, is it worth the trouble? Everybody who has ever been within fifty miles of the falls has written his or her impressions. Everybody who has never seen the falls knows all about them, and—besides, I want some more apples. They're good in this place, ye big fat man," I quoted.

The Professor retired into his hammock for a while. Then he reappeared flushed with a new thought. "If you want to see something quite new let's go to Chautauqua."

"What's that?"

"Well, it's a sort of institution. It's an educational idea, and it lives on the borders of a lake in New York State. I think you'll find it interesting; and I know it will show you a new side of American life."

In blank ignorance I consented. Everybody is anxious that I should see as many sides of American life as possible. Here in the East they demand of me what I thought of their West. I dare not answer that it is as far from their notions and motives as Hindustan from Hoboken—that the West, to this poor thinking, is an America which has no kinship with its neighbour. Therefore I congratulated them hypocritically upon "their West," and from their lips learn that there is yet another America, that of the South—alien and distinct. Into the third country, alas! I shall not have time to penetrate. The newspapers and the oratory of the day will tell you that all feeling between the North and South is extinct. None the less the Northerner, outside his newspapers and public men, has a healthy contempt for the Southerner which the latter repays by what seems very like a deep-rooted aversion to the Northerner. I have learned now what the sentiments of the great American nation mean. The North speaks in the name of the country; the West is busy developing its own resources, and the Southerner skulks in his tents. His opinions do not count; but his girls are very beautiful.

So the Professor and I took a train and went to look at the educational idea. From sleepy, quiet little Musquash we rattled through the coal and iron districts of Pennsylvania, her coke ovens flaring into the night and her clamorous foundries waking the silence of the woods in which they lay. Twenty years hence woods and cornfields will be gone, and from Pittsburg to Shenango all will be smoky black as Bradford and Beverly: for each factory is drawing to itself a small town, and year by year the demand for rails increases. The Professor held forth on the labour question, his remarks being prompted by the sight of a train-load of Italians and Hungarians going home from mending a bridge.

"You recollect the Burmese," said he. "The American is like the Burman in one way. He won't do heavy manual labour. He knows too much. Consequently he imports the alien to be his hands—just as the Burman gets hold of the Madrassi. If he shuts down all labour immigration he will have to fill up his own dams, cut his cuttings and pile his own embankments. The American citizen won't like that. He is racially unfit to be a labourer in muttee. He can invent, buy, sell and design, but he cannot waste his time on earthworks. Iswaste, this great people will resume contract labour immigration the minute they find the aliens in their midst are not sufficient for the jobs in hand. If the alien gives them trouble they will shoot him."

"Yes, they will shoot him," I said, remembering how only two days before some Hungarians employed on a line near Musquash had seen fit to strike and to roll down rocks on labourers hired to take their places, an amusement which caused the sheriff to open fire with a revolver and wound or kill (it really does not much matter which) two or three of them. Only a man who earns ten pence a day in sunny Italy knows how to howl for as many shillings in America.

The composition of the crowd in the cars began to attract my attention. There were very many women and a few clergymen. Where you shall find these two together, there also shall be a fad, a hobby, a theory, or a mission.

"These people are going to Chautauqua," said the Professor. "It's a sort of open-air college—they call it—but you'll understand things better when you arrive." A grim twinkle in the back of his eye awakened all my fears.

"Can you get anything to drink there?"

"No."

"Are you allowed to smoke?"

"Ye-es, in certain places."

"Are we staying there over Sunday?"

"No." This very emphatically.

Feminine shrieks of welcome: "There's Sadie!" "Why, Maimie, is that yeou!" "Alfs in the smoker. Did you bring the baby?" and a profligate expenditure of kisses between bonnet and bonnet told me we had struck a gathering place of the clans. It was midnight. They swept us, this horde of clamouring women, into a Black Maria omnibus and a sumptuous hotel close to the borders of a lake—Lake Chautauqua. Morning showed as pleasant a place of summer pleasuring as ever I wish to see. Smooth-cut lawns of velvet grass, studded with tennis-courts, surrounded the hotel and ran down to the blue waters, which were dotted with rowboats. Young men in wonderful blazers, and maidens in more wonderful tennis costumes; women attired with all the extravagance of unthinking Chicago or the grace of Washington (which is Simla) filled the grounds, and the neat French nurses and exquisitely dressed little children ran about together. There was pickerel-fishing for such as enjoyed it; a bowling-alley, unlimited bathing and a toboggan, besides many other amusements, all winding up with a dance or a concert at night. Women dominated the sham mediæval hotel, rampaged about the passages, flirted in the corridors and chased unruly children off the tennis-courts. This place was called Lakewood. It is a pleasant place for the unregenerate,

"We go up the lake in a steamer to Chautauqua," said the Professor,

"But I want to stay here. This is what I understand and like."

"No, you don't. You must come along and be educated."

All the shores of the lake, which is eighteen miles long, are dotted with summer hotels, camps, boathouses and pleasant places of rest. You go there with all your family to fish and to flirt. There is no special beauty in the landscape of tame cultivated hills and decorous, woolly trees, but good taste and wealth have taken the place in hand, trimmed its borders and made it altogether delightful.

The institution of Chautauqua is the largest village on the lake. I can't hope to give you an idea of it, but try to imagine the Charlesville at Mussoorie magnified ten times and set down in the midst of hundreds of tiny little hill houses, each different from its neighbour, brightly painted and constructed of wood. Add something of the peace of dull Dalhousie, flavour with a tincture of missions and the old Polytechnic, Cassell's Self Educator and a Monday pop, and spread the result out flat on the shores of Naini Tal Lake, which you will please transport to the Dun. But that does not half describe the idea. We watched it through a wicket gate, where we were furnished with a red ticket, price forty cents, and five dollars if you lost it. I naturally lost mine on the spot and was fined accordingly.

Once inside the grounds on the paths that serpentined round the myriad cottages I was lost in admiration of scores of pretty girls, most of them with little books under their arms, and a pretty air of seriousness on their faces. Then I stumbled upon an elaborately arranged mass of artificial hillocks surrounding a mud puddle and a wormy streak of slime connecting it with another mud puddle. Little boulders topped with square pieces of putty were strewn over the hillocks—evidently with intention. When I hit my foot against one such boulder painted "Jericho," I demanded information in aggrieved tones.

"Hsh!" said the Professor. "It's a model of Palestine—the Holy Land—done to scale and all that, you know."

Two young people were flirting on the top of the highest mountain overlooking Jerusalem; the mud puddles were meant for the Dead Sea and the Sea of Galilee, and the twisting gutter was the Jordan. A small boy sat on the city "Safed" and cast his line into Chautauqua Lake. On the whole it did not impress me. The hotel was filled with women, and a large blackboard in the main hall set forth the exercises for the day. It seemed that Chautauqua was a sort of educational syndicate, cum hotel, cum (very mild) Rosherville. There were annually classes of young women and young men who studied in the little cottages for two or three months in the year and went away to self-educate themselves. There were other classes who learned things by correspondence, and yet other classes made up the teachers. All these delights I had missed, but had arrived just in time for a sort of debauch of lectures which concluded the three months' education. The syndicate in control had hired various lecturers whose names would draw audiences, and these men were lecturing about the labour problem, the servant-girl question, the artistic and political aspect of Greek life, the Pope in the Middle Ages and similar subjects, in all of which young women do naturally take deep delight. Professor Mahaffy (what the devil was he doing in that gallery?) was the Greek art side man, and a Dr. Gunsaulus handled the Pope. The latter I loved forthwith. He had been to some gathering on much the same lines as the Chautauqua one, and had there been detected, in the open daylight, smoking a cigar. One whole lighted cigar. Then his congregation or his class, or the mothers of both of them, wished to know whether this was the sort of conduct for a man professing temperance. I have not heard Dr. Gunsaulus lecture, but he must be a good man. Professor Mahaffy was enjoying himself. I sat close to him at tiffin and heard him arguing with an American professor as to the merits of the American Constitution. Both men spoke that the table might get the benefit of their wisdom, whence I argued that even eminent professors are eminently human.

"Now, for goodness' sake, behave yourself," said the Professor. "You are not to ask the whereabouts of a bar. You are not to laugh at anything you see, and you are not to go away and deride this Institution."

Remember that advice. But I was virtuous throughout, and my virtue brought its own reward. The parlour of the hotel was full of committees of women; some of them were Methodist Episcopalians, some were Congregationalists, and some were United Presbyterians; and some were faith healers and Christian Scientists, and all trotted about with notebooks in their hands and the expression of Atlas on their faces. They were connected with missions to the heathen, and so forth, and their deliberations appeared to be controlled by a male missionary. The Professor introduced me to one of them as their friend from India.

"Indeed," said she; "and of what denomination are you?"

"I—I live in India," I murmured.

"You are a missionary, then?"

I had obeyed the Professor's orders all too well. "I am not a missionary," I said, with, I trust, a decent amount of regret in my tones. She dropped me and I went to find the Professor, who had cowardly deserted me, and I think was laughing on the balcony. It is very hard to persuade a denominational American that a man from India is not a missionary. The home-returned preachers very naturally convey the impression that India is inhabited solely by missionaries.

I heard some of them telling and saw how, all unconsciously, they were hinting the thing which was not. But prejudice governs me against my will. When a woman looks you in the face and pities you for having to associate with "heathen" and "idolaters"—Sikh Sirdar of the north, if you please, Mahommedan gentlemen and the simple-minded Jat of the Punjab—what can you do?

The Professor took me out to see the sights, and lest I should be further treated as a denominational missionary I wrapped myself in tobacco smoke. This ensures respectful treatment at Chautauqua. An amphitheatre capable of seating five thousand people is the centre-point of the show. Here the lecturers lecture and the concerts are held, and from here the avenues start. Each cottage is decorated according to the taste of the owner, and is full of girls. The verandahs are alive with them; they fill the sinuous walks; they hurry from lecture to lecture, hatless, and three under one sunshade; they retail little confidences walking arm-in-arm; they giggle for all the world like uneducated maidens, and they walk about and row on the lake with their very young men. The lectures are arranged to suit all tastes. I got hold of one called "The Eschatology of Our Saviour." It set itself to prove the length, breadth and temperature of Hell from information garnered from the New Testament. I read it in the sunshine under the trees, with these hundreds of pretty maidens pretending to be busy all round; and it did not seem to match the landscape. Then I studied the faces of the crowd. One-quarter were old and worn; the balance were young, innocent, charming and frivolous. I wondered how much they really knew or cared for the art side of Greek life, or the Pope in the Middle Ages; and how much for the young men who walked with them. Also what their ideas of Hell might be. We entered a place called a museum (all the shows here are of an improving tendency) , which had evidently been brought together by feminine hands, so jumbled were the exhibits. There was a facsimile of the Rosetta stone, with some printed popular information; an Egyptian camel saddle, miscellaneous truck from the Holy Land, another model of the same, photographs of Rome, badly-blotched drawings of volcanic phenomena, the head of the pike that John Brown took to Harper's Ferry that time his soul went marching on, casts of doubtful value, and views of Chautauqua, all bundled together without the faintest attempt at arrangement, and all very badly labelled.

It was the apotheosis of Popular Information. I told the Professor so, and he said I was an ass, which didn't affect the statement in the least. I have seen museums like Chautauqua before, and well I know what they mean. If you do not understand, read the first part of Aurora Leigh. Lectures on the Chautauqua stamp I have heard before. People don't get educated that way. They must dig for it, and cry for it, and sit up o' nights for it; and when they have got it they must call it by another name or their struggle is of no avail. You can get a degree from this Lawn Tennis Tabernacle of all the arts and sciences at Chautauqua. Mercifully the students are womenfolk, and if they marry the degree is forgotten, and if they become school-teachers they can only instruct young America in the art of mispronouncing his own language. And yet so great is the perversity of the American girl that she can, scorning tennis and the allurements of boating, work herself nearly to death over the skittles of archaeology and foreign tongues, to the sorrow of all her friends.

Late that evening the contemptuous courtesy of the hotel allotted me a room in a cottage of quarter-inch planking, destitute of the most essential articles of toilette furniture. Ten shillings a day was the price of this shelter, for Chautauqua is a paying institution. I heard the Professor next door banging about like a big jack-rabbit in a very small packing-case. Presently he entered, holding between disgusted finger and thumb the butt end of a candle, his only light, and this in a house that would bum quicker than cardboard if once lighted.

"Isn't it shameful? Isn't it atrocious? A dâk bungalow khansamah wouldn't dare to give me a raw candle to go to bed by. I say, when you describe this hole rend them to pieces. A candle stump! Give it 'em hot."

You will remember the Professor's advice to me not long ago. "'Fessor," said I loftily (my own room was a windowless dog-kennel) , "this is unseemly. We are now in the most civilised country on earth, enjoying the advantages of an Institootion which is the flower of the civilisation of the nineteenth century; and yet you kick up a fuss over being obliged to go to bed by the stump of a candle! Think of the Pope in the Middle Ages. Reflect on the art side of Greek life. Remember the Sabbath day to keep it holy, and get out of this. You're filling two-thirds of my room."

Apropos of Sabbath, I have come across some lovely reading which it grieves me that I have not preserved. Chautauqua, you must know, shuts down on Sundays. With awful severity an eminent clergyman has been writing to the papers about the beauties of the system. The stalls that dispense terrible drinks of Moxie, typhoidal milk-shakes and sulphuric-acid-on-lime-bred soda-water are stopped; boating is forbidden; no steamer calls at the jetty, and the nearest railway station is three miles off, and you can't hire a conveyance; the barbers must not shave you, and no milkman or butcher goes his rounds. The reverend gentleman enjoys this (he must wear a beard). I forget his exact words, but they run: "And thus, thank God, no one can supply himself on the Lord's day with the luxuries or conveniences that he has neglected to procure on Saturday," Of course, if you happen to linger inside the wicket gate—verily Chautauqua is a close preserve—over Sunday, you must bow gracefully to the rules of the place. But what are you to do with this frame of mind? The owner of it would send missions to convert the "heathen," or would convert you at ten minutes' notice; and yet if you called him a heathen and an idolater he would probably be very much offended.

Oh, my friends, I have been to one source of the river of missionary enterprise, and the waters thereof are bitter—bitter as hate, narrow as the grave! Not now do I wonder that the missionary in the East is at times, to our thinking, a little intolerant towards beliefs he cannot understand and people he does not appreciate. Rather it is a mystery to me that these delegates of an imperious ecclesiasticism have not a hundred times ere this provoked murder and fire among our wards. If they were true to the iron teachings of Centreville or Petumna or Chunkhaven, when they came they would have done so. For Centreville or Smithson or Squeehawken teach the only true creeds in all the world, and to err from their tenets, as laid down by the bishops and the elders, is damnation. How it may be in England at the centres of supply I cannot tell, but shall presently learn. Here in America I am afraid of these grim men of the denominations, who know so intimately the will of the Lord and enforce it to the uttermost. Left to themselves they would prayerfully, in all good faith and sincerity, slide gradually, ere a hundred years, from the mental inquisitions which they now work with some success to an institootion—be sure it would be an "institootion" with a journal of its own—not far different from what the Torquemada ruled aforetime. Does this seem extravagant? I have watched the expression on the men's faces when they told me that they would rather see their son or daughter dead at their feet than doing such and such things—trampling on the grass on a Sunday, or something equally heinous—and I was grateful that the law of men stood between me and their interpretation of the law of God. They would assuredly slay the body for the soul's sake and account it righteousness. And this would befall not in the next generation, perhaps, but in the next, for the very look I saw in a Eusufzai's face at Peshawar when he turned and spat in my tracks I have seen this day at Chautauqua in the face of a preacher. The will was there, but not the power.

The Professor went up the lake on a visit, taking my ticket of admission with him, and I found a child, aged seven, fishing with a worm and pin, and spent the rest of the afternoon in his company. He was a delightful young citizen, full of information and apparently ignorant of denominations. We caught sunfish and catfish and pickerel together.

The trouble began when I attempted to escape through the wicket on the jetty and let the creeds fight it out among themselves. Without that ticket I could not go, unless I paid five dollars. That was the rule to prevent people cheating.

"You see," quoth a man in charge, "you've no idea of the meanness of these people. Why, there was a lady this season—a prominent member of the Baptist connection—we know, but we can't prove it that she had two of her hired girls in a cellar when the grounds were being canvassed for the annual poll-tax of five dollars a head. So she saved ten dollars. We can't be too careful with this crowd. You've got to produce that ticket as a proof that you haven't been living in the grounds for weeks and weeks."

"For weeks and weeks!" The blue went out of the sky as he said it. "But I wouldn't stay here for one week if I could help it," I answered.

"No more would I," he said earnestly.

Returned the Professor in a steamer, and him I basely left to make explanations about that ticket, while I returned to Lakewood—the nice hotel without any regulations. I feared that I should be kept in those terrible grounds for the rest of my life.

And it turned out an hour later that the same fear lay upon the Professor also. He arrived heated but exultant, having baffled the combined forces of all the denominations and recovered the five-dollar deposit. "I wouldn't go inside those gates for anything," he said. "I waited on the jetty. What do you think of it all?'

"It has shown me a new side of American life," I responded. "I never want to see it again—and I'm awfully sorry for the girls who take it seriously. I suppose the bulk of them don't. They just have a good time. But it would be better—"

"How?"

"If they all got married instead of pumping up interest in a bric-a-brac museum and advertised lectures, and having their names in the papers. One never gets to believe in the proper destiny of woman until one sees a thousand of 'em doing something different. I don't like Chautauqua. There's something wrong with it, and I haven't time to find out where. But it is wrong."

The Bow Flume Cable-Car

"See those things yonder?" He looked in the direction of the Market Street cable-cars which, moved without any visible agency, were conveying the good people of San Francisco to a picnic somewhere across the harbour. The stranger was not more than seven feet high. His face was burnished copper, his hands and beard were fiery red and his eyes a baleful blue. He had thrust his large frame into a suit of black clothes which made no pretensions toward fitting him, and his cheek was distended with plug-tobacco. "Those cars," he said, more to himself than to me, "run upon a concealed cable worked by machinery, and that's what broke our sindicate at Bow Flume. Concealed machinery, no—concealed ropes. Don't you mix yourself with them. They are not trustworthy."

"These cars work comfortably," I ventured. "They run over people now and then, but that doesn't matter."

"Certainly not, not in 'Frisco—by no means. It's different out yonder." He waved a palmleaf fan in the direction of Mission Dolores among the sandhills. Then without a moment's pause, and in a low and melancholy voice, he continued: "Young feller, all patent machinery is a monopoly, and don't you try to bust it or else it will bust you. 'Bout five years ago I was at Bow Flume—a minin'-town way back yonder—beyond the Sacramento. I ran a saloon there with O'Grady—Howlin' O'Grady, so called on account of the noise he made when intoxicated. I never christened my saloon any high-soundin' name, but owing to my happy trick of firing out men who was too full of bug-juice and disposed to be promiscuous in their dealin's, the boys called it 'The Wake Up an' Git Bar.' O'Grady, my partner, was an unreasonable inventorman. He invented a check on the whisky bar'ls that wasn't no good except lettin' the whisky run off at odd times and shutting down when a man was most thirstiest. I remember half Bow Flume city firing their six-shooters into a cask—and Bourbon at that—which was refusing to run on account of O'Grady's patent doublecheck tap. But that wasn't what I started to tell you about—not by a long ways. O'Grady went to 'Frisco when the Bow Flume saloon was booming. He hed a good time in 'Frisco, kase he came back with a very bad head and no clothes worth talkin' about. He had been jailed most time, but he had investigated the mechanism of these cars yonder—when he wasn't in the cage. He came back with the liquor for the saloon, and the boys whooped round him for half a day, singing songs of glory. 'Boys,' says O'Grady, when a half of Bow Flume were lying on the floor kissing the cuspidors and singing 'Way Down the Swanee River,' being full of some new stuff O'Grady had got up from 'Frisco—'boys,' says O'Grady, 'I have the makings of a company in me. You know the road from this saloon to Bow Flimie is bad and 'most perpendicular.' That was the exact state of the case. Bow Flume city was three hundred feet above our saloon. The boys used to roll down and get full, and any that happened to be sober rolled them up again when the time came to get. Some dropped into the cañon that way—bad payers mostly. You see, a man held all the hill Bow Flume was built on, and he wanted forty thousand dollars for a forty-five by hundred lot o' ground. We kept the whisky and the boys came down for it. The exercise disposed them to thirst. 'Boys,' says O'Grady, 'as you know, I have visited the great metropolis of 'Frisco.' Then they had drinks all round for 'Frisco. 'And I have been jailed a few while enjoying the sights.' Then they had drinks all round for the jail that held O'Grady. 'But,' he says, 'I have a proposal to make.' More drinks on account of the proposal. 'I have got a hold of the idea of those 'Frisco cable-cars. Some of the idea I got in 'Frisco. The rest I have invented,' says O'Grady. Then they drank all round for the invention.

"I am coming to the point. O'Grady made a company—the drunkest I ever saw—to run a cable-car on the 'Frisco model from 'Wake Up an' Git Saloon' to Bow Flume. The boys put in about four thousand dollars, for Bow Flume was squirling gold then. There's nary shanty there now. O'Grady put in four thousand dollars of his own, and I was roped in for as much. O'Grady desired the concern to represent the resources of Bow Flume. We got a car built in 'Frisco for two thousand dollars, with an elegant bar at one end—nickelplated fixings and ruby glass.

"The notion was to dispense liquor en route. A Bow Flume man could put himself outside two drinks in a minute and a half, the same not being pressed for urgent business. The boys graded the road for love, and we run a rope in a little trough in the middle. That rope ran swift, and any blame fool that had his foot cut off, fooling in the middle of the road, might ha' found salvation by using our Bow Flume Palace Car. The boys said that was square. O'Grady took the contract for building the engine to wind the rope. He called his show a mule—it was a crossbreed between a threshing machine and an elevator ram. I don't think he had followed the 'Frisco patterns. He put all our dollars into that blamed barroom on the car, knowing what would please the boys best. They didn't care much about the machinery, so long as the car hummed.

"We charged the boys a dollar a head per trip. One free drink included. That paid—paid like—Paradise. They liked the motion. O'Grady was engineer, and another man sort of tended to the rope engine when he wasn't otherwise engaged. Those cable-cars run by gripping on to the rope. You know that. When the grip's off the car is braked down and stands still. There ought to have been two cars by right—one to run up and the other down. But O'Grady had a blamed invention for reversing the engine, so the cable ran both ways—up to Bow Flimie and down to the saloon—the terminus being in front of our door. A man could kick a friend slick from the bar into the car. The boys appreciated that. The Bow Flume Palace Car Company earned twenty on the hundred in three months, besides the profit on the drinks. We might have lasted to this days if O'Grady hadn' tinkered his blamed engine on to of Bow Flume Hill. The boys complained the show didn't hum sufficient. They required railroad speed. O'Grady ran 'em up and down at fourteen miles an hour; and his latest improvement was to touch twenty-four. The strain on the brakes was terrible—quite terrible. But every time O'Grady raised the record, the boys gave him a testimonial. 'Twasn't in human nature not to crowd ahead after that. Testimonials demorilse the publickest of men.

"I rode in the car that memorial day. Just as we started with a double load of boys and a razzle-dazzle assortment of drinks, something went zip under the car bottom. All the prominent members of the company were aboard. 'The grip has got snubbed on the rope,' says O'Grady quite quietly. 'Boys, this will be the biggest smash on record. Something's going to happen.' We proceeded at the rate of twenty-four miles an hour till the end of our journey. I don't know what happened there. We could get clear of the rope anyways at the point where it turned round a pulley to start up hill again. We struck—struck the stoop of the 'Wake Up an' Git Saloon'—my saloon—and the next thing I knew was feeling of my legs under an assortment of matchwood and broken glass, representing liquor and fixtures to the tune of eight thousand. The car had been flicked through the saloon, bringing down the entire roof on the floor. It had then bucked out into the firmament, describing a parabola over the bluff at the back of the saloon, and was lying at the foot of that bluff, three hundred feet below, like a busted kaleidoscope—all nickel, shavings and bits of red glass. O'Grady and most of the prominent members of the company were dead—very dead—and there wasn't enough left of the saloon to pay for a drink.

I took in the situation lying on my stomach at the edge of the bluff, and I suspicioned that any lawsuits that might arise would be complicated by shooting. So I quit Bow Flume by the back trail. I guess the coroner judged that there were no summons—leastways I never heard any more about it. Since that time I've had a distrust to cable-cars. The rope breaking is no great odds, bekase you can stop the car, but it's getting the grip tangled with the running rope that spreads ruin and desolation over thriving communities and prevents the development of local resources."

In Partibus

The 'buses run to Battersea,
The 'buses run to Bow,
The 'buses run to Westbourne Grove,
And Nottinghill also;
But I am sick of London town.
From Shepherd's Bush to Bow.

I see the smut upon my cuff
And feel him on my nose;
I cannot leave my window wide
When gentle zephyr blows,

Because he brings disgusting things
And drops 'em on my "clo'es."

The sky, a greasy soup-toureen.
Shuts down atop my brow.
Yes, I have sighed for London town
And I have got it now:
And half of it is fog and filth.
And half is fog and row.

And when I take my nightly prowl,
'Tis passing good to meet
The pious Briton lugging home
His wife and daughter sweet,
Through four packed miles of seething vice.
Thrust out upon the street.

Earth holds no horror like to this
In any land displayed.
From Suez unto Sandy Hook,
From Calais to Port Said;
And 'twas to hide their heathendom
The beastly fog was made.

I cannot tell when dawn is near,
Or when the day is done.
Because I always see the gas
And never see the sun.
And now, methinks, I do not care
A cuss for either one.

But stay, there was an orange, or
An aged egg its yolk;
It might have been a Pears' balloon
Or Barnum's latest joke:
I took it for the sun and wept
To watch it through the smoke.

It's Oh to see the morn ablaze
Above the mango-tope,
When homeward through the dewy cane
The little jackals lope.
And half Bengal heaves into view.
New-washed—with sunlight soap.

It's Oh for one deep whisky peg
When Christmas winds are blowing.
When all the men you ever knew.

And all you've ceased from knowing.
Are "entered for the Tournament,
And everything that's going."

But I consort with long-haired things
In velvet collar-rolls.
Who talk about the Aims of Art,
And "theories" and "goals,"
And moo and coo with women-folk
About their blessed souls.

But that they call "psychology"
Is lack of liver pill,
And all that blights their tender souls
Is eating till they're ill,
And their chief way of winning goals
Consists in sitting still.

It's Oh to meet an Army man.
Set up, and trimmed and taut.
Who does not spout hashed libraries
Or think the next man's thought.
And walks as though he owned himself.
And hogs his bristles short.

Hear now, a voice across the seas
To kin beyond my ken,
If ye have ever filled an hour
With stories from my pen.
For pity's sake send some one here
To bring me news of men!

The 'buses run to Islington,
To Highgate and Soho,
To Hammersmith and Kew therewith.
And Camberwell also.
But I can only murmur "'Buss"
From Shepherd's Bush to Bow.

Letters On Leave

I

To Lieutenant John McHail,
151st (Kumharsen) P.N.I.,
Hakaiti via Tharanda,

Assam.

DEAR OLD MAN: Your handwriting is worse than ever, but as far as I can see among the loops and fish-hooks, you are lonesome and want to be comforted with a letter. I knew you wouldn't write to me unless you needed something. You don't tell me that you have left your regiment, but from what you say about "my battalion," "my men," and so forth, it seems as if you were raising military police for the benefit of the Chins. If that's the case, I congratulate you. The pay is good. Ouless writes to me from some new fort something or other, saying that he has struggled into a billet of Rs. 700 (Military Police), and instead of being chased by writters as he used to be, is ravaging the country round Shillong in search of a wife. I am very sorry for the Mrs. Ouless of the future.

That doesn't matter. You probably know more about the boys yonder than I do. If you'll only send me from time to time some record of their movements I'll try to tell you of things on this side of the water. You say "You don't know what it is to hear from town." I say "You don't know what it is to hear from the dehat," Now and again men drift in with news, but I don't like hot-weather khubber. It's all of the domestic occurrence kind. Old "Hat" Constable came to see me the other day. You remember the click in his throat before he begins to speak. He sat still, clicking at quarter-hour intervals, and after each click he'd say: "D'ye remember Mistress So-an'-So? Well, she's dead o' typhoid at Naogong." When it wasn't "Mistress So-an'-So" it was a man. I stood four clicks and four deaths, and then I asked him to spare me the rest. You seem to have had a bad season, taking it all round, and the women seem to have suffered most. Is that so?

We don't die in London. We go out of town, and we make as much fuss about it as if we were going to the Neva. Now I understand why the transport is the first thing to break down when our army takes the field. The Englishman is cumbrous in his movements and very particular about his baskets and hampers and trunks—not less than seven of each—for a fifty-mile journey. Leave season began some weeks ago, and there is a burra-choop along the streets that you could shovel with a spade. All the people that say they are everybody have gone—quite two hundred miles away. Some of 'em are even on the Continent—and the clubs are full of strange folk. I found a Reform man at the Savage a week ago. He didn't say what his business was, but he was dusty and looked hungry. I suppose he had come in for food and shelter.

Like the rest I'm on leave too. I converted myself into a Government Secretary, awarded myself one month on full pay with the chance of an extension, and went off. Then it rained and hailed, and rained again, and I ran up and down this tiny country in trains trying to find a dry place. After ten days I came back to town, having been stopped by the sea four times. I was rather like a kitten at the bottom of a bucke chasing its own tail. So I'm sitting here under a grey, muggy sky wondering what sort of time they are having at Simla. It's August now. The rains would be nearly over, all the theatricals would be in full swing, and Jakko Hill would be just Paradise. You're probably pink with prickly heat. Sit down quietly under the punkah and think of Umballa station, hot as an oven at four in the morning. Think of the dak-gharry slobbering in the wet, and the first little cold wind that comes round the first comer after the tonga is clear of Kalka. There's a wind you and I know well. It's blowing over the grass at Dugshai this very moment, and there's a smell of hot fir trees all along and along from Solon to Simla, and some happy man is flying up that road with fragments of a tonga-bar in his eye, his pet terrier under his arm, his thick clothes on the back-seat and the certainty of a month's pure joy in front of him. Instead of which you're being stewed at Hakaiti and I'm sitting in a second-hand atmosphere above a sausage-shop, watching three sparrows playing in a dirty-green tree and pretending that it's summer, I have a view of very many streets and a river. Except the advertisements on the walls, there isn't one speck of colour as far as my eye can reach. The very cat, who is an amiable beast, comes off black under my hand, and I daren't open the window for fear of smuts. And this is better than a soaked and sobbled country, with the corn-shocks standing like plover's eggs in green moss and the oats lying flat in moist lumps. We haven't had any summer, and yesterday I smelt the raw touch of the winter. Just one little whiff to show that the year had turned. "Oh, what a happy land is England!"

I cannot understand the white man at home. You remember when we went out together and landed at the Apollo Bunder with all our sorrows before us, and went to Watson's Hotel and saw the snake-charmers? You said: "It'll take me all my lifetime to distinguish one nigger from another." That was eight years ago. Now you don't call them niggers any more, and you're supposed—quite wrongly—to have an insight into native character, or else you would never have been allowed to recruit for the Kumharsens. I feel as I felt at Watson's. They are so deathlily alike, especially the more educated. They all seem to read the same books, and the same newspapers telling 'em what to admire in the same books, and they all quote the same passages from the same books, and they write books on books about somebody else's books, and they are penetrated to their boot-heels with a sense of the awful seriousness of their own views of the moment. Above that they seem to be, most curiously and beyond the right of ordinary people, divorced from the knowledge or fear of death. Of course, every man conceives that every man except himself is bound to die (you remember how Hallatt spoke the night before he went out), but these men appear to be like children in that respect.

I can't explain exactly, but it gives an air of unreality to their most earnest earnestnesses; and when a young man of views and culture and aspirations is in earnest, the trumpets of Jericho are silent beside him. Because they have everything done for them they know how everything ought to be done; and they are perfectly certain that wood pavements, policemen, shops and gaslight come in the regular course of nature. You can guess with these convictions how thoroughly and cocksurely they handle little trifles like colonial administration, the wants of the army, municipal sewage, housing of the poor, and so forth. Every third common need of average men is, in their mouths, a tendency or a movement or a federation affecting the world. It never seems to occur to 'em that the human instinct of getting as much as possible for money paid, or, failing money, for threats and fawnings, is about as old as Cain; and the burden of their bat is: "Me an' a few mates o' mine are going to make a new world."

As long as men only write and talk they must think that way, I suppose. It's compensation for playing with little things. And that reminds me. Do you know the University smile? You don't by that name, but sometimes young civilians wear it for a very short time when they first come out. Something—I wonder if it's our brutal chaff, or a billiard-cue, or which?—takes it out of their faces, and when they next differ with you they do so without smiling. But that smile flourishes in London. I've met it again and again. It expresses tempered grief, sorrow at your complete inability to march with the march of progress at the Universities, and a chastened contempt. There is one man who wears it as a garment. He is frivolously young—not more than thirty-five or forty—and all these years no one has removed that smile. He knows everything about everything on this earth, and above all he knows all about men under any and every condition of life. He knows all about the aggressive militarism of you and your friends; he isn't quite sure of the necessity of an army; he is certain that colonial expansion is nonsense; and he is more than certain that the whole step of all our Empire must be regulated by the knowledge and foresight of the workingman. Then he smiles—smiles like a seraph with an M.A. degree. What can you do with a man like that? He has never seen an unmade road in his life; I think he believes that wheat grows on a tree and that beef is dug from a mine. He has never been forty miles from a railway, and he has never been called upon to issue an order to anybody except his well-fed servants. Isn't it wondrous? And there are battalions and brigades of these men in town removed from the fear of want, living until they are seventy or eighty, sheltered, fed, drained and administered, expending their vast leisure in talking and writing.

|

But the real fun begins much lower down the line. I've been associating generally and very particularly with the men who say that they are the only men in the world who work—and they call themselves the workingman. Now the workingman in America is a nice person. He says he is a man and behaves accordingly. That is to say, he has some notion that he is part and parcel of a great country. At least, he talks that way. But in this town you can see thousands of men meeting publicly on Sundays to cry aloud that everybody may hear that they are poor, downtrodden helots—in fact, "the pore workin' man." At their clubs and pubs the talk is the same. It's the utter want of self-respect that revolts. My friend the tobacconist has a cousin, who is, apparently, sound in mind and limb, aged twenty-three, clear-eyed and upstanding. He is a "skibbo" by trade—a painter of sorts. He married at twenty, and he has two children. He can spend three-quarters of an hour talking about his downtrodden condition. He works under another Raj-mistri, who has saved money and started a little shop of his own. He hates that Raj-mistri; he loathes the police; and his views on the lives and customs of the aristocracy are strange. He approves of every form of lawlessness, and he knows that everybody who holds authority is sure to be making a good thing out of it. Of himself as a citizen he never thinks. Of himself as an Ishmael he thinks a good deal. He is entitled to eight hours' work a day and some time off—said time to be paid for; he is entitled to free education for his children—and he doesn't want no bloomin' clergyman to teach 'em; he is entitled to houses especially built for himself because he pays the bulk of the taxes of the country. He is not going to emigrate, not he; he reserves to himself the right of multiplying as much as he pleases; the streets must be policed for him while he demonstrates, immediately under my window, by the way, for ten consecutive hours, and I am probably a thief because my dothes are better than his. The proposition is a very simple one. He has no duties to the State, no personal responsibility of any kind, and he'd sooner see his children dead than soldiers of the Queen. The Government owes him everything because he is a pore workin'man. When the Guards tried their Board-school mutiny at the Wellington Barracks my friend was jubilant. "What did I tell your he said. "You see the very soldiers won't stand it."

"What's it?"

"Bein' treated like machines instead of flesh and blood. 'Course they won't."

The popular evening paper wrote that the Guards, with perfect justice, had rebelled against being treated like machines instead of flesh and blood. Then I thought of a certain regiment that lay in Mian Mir for three years and dropped four hundred men out of a thousand. It died of fever and cholera. There were no pretty nursemaids to work with it in the streets, because there were no streets. I saw how the Guards amused themselves and how their sergeants smoked in uniform. I pitied the Guards with their cruel sentry-goes, their three nights out of bed, and their unlimited supply of love and liquor.

Another man, not a workman, told me that the Guards' riot—it's impossible, as you know, to call this kick-up of the fatted flunkies of the army a mutiny—was only "a schoolboy's prank"; and he could not see that if it was what he said it was, the Guards were no regiment and should have been wiped out decently and quietly. There again the futility of a sheltered people cropped up. You mustn't treat a man like a machine in this country, but you can't get any work out of a man till he has learned to work like a machine. D— has just come home for a few months from the charge of a mountain battery on the frontier. He used to begin work at eight, and he was thankful if he got off at six; most of the time on his feet. When he went to the Black Mountain he was extensively engaged for nearly sixteen hours a day; and that on food at which the "pore workin' man" would have turned up his state-lifted nose. D— on the subject of labour as understood by the white man in his own home is worth hearing. Though coarse—considerably coarse! But D— doesn't know all the hopeless misery of the business. When the small pig, oyster, furniture, carpet, builder or general shopman works his way out of the ruck he turns round and makes his old friends and employees sweat. He knows how near he can go to flaying 'em alive before they kick; and in this matter he is neither better nor worse than a bunnia or a havildar of our own blessed country. It's the small employer of labour that skins his servant, exactly as the forty-pound householder works her one white servant to the bone and goes to drop pennies into the plate to convert the heathen in the East.

Just at present, as you have read, the person who calls himself the pore workin' man—the man I saw kicking fallen men in the mud by the docks last winter—has discovered a real, fine, new original notion; and he is working it for all he is worth. He calls it the solidarity of labour bundobast; but it's caste—four thousand years old, caste of Menu—with old shetts, mahajuns, guildtolls, excommunication and all the rest of it. All things considered, there isn't anything much older than caste—it began with the second generation of man on earth—but to read the "advance" papers on the subject you'd imagine it was a revelation from Heaven. The real fun will begin—as it has begun and ended many times before—when the caste of skilled labour—that's the pore workin' man—are pushed up and knocked about by the lower and unrecognised castes, who will form castes of their own and outcaste on the decision of their own punchayats. How these castes will scuffle and fight among themselves, and how astonished the Englishman will be!

He is naturally lawless because he is a fighting animal; and his amazingly sheltered condition has made him inconsequent. I don't like inconsequent lawlessness. I've seen it down at Bow Street, at the docks, by the G.P.O., and elsewhere. Its chief home, of course, is in that queer place called the House of Commons, but no one goes there who isn't forced by business. It's shut up at present, and the persons who belong to it are loose all over the face of the country, I don't think—but I won't swear—that any of them are spitting at policemen. One man appears to have been poaching, others are advocating various forms of murder and outrage—and nobody seems to care. The residue talk—just heavens, how they talk, and what wonderful fictions they tell! And they firmly believe, being ignorant of the mechanism of Government, that they administer the country. In addition, certain of their newspapers have elaborately worked up a famine in Ireland that could be engineered by two Deputy Commissioners and four average Stunts into a "woe" and a "calamity" that is going to overshadow the peace of the nation—even the Empire. I suppose they have their own sense of proportion, but they manage to keep it to themselves very successfully. What do you, who have seen half a countryside in deadly fear of its life, suppose that this people would do if they were chukkered and gabraowed? If they really knew what the fear of death and the dread of injury implied? If they died very swiftly, indeed, and could not count their futile lives enduring beyond next sundown? Some of the men from your—I mean our—part of the world say that they would be afraid and break and scatter and run. But there is no room in the island to run. The sea catches you, midwaist, at the third step. I am curious to see if the cholera, of which these people stand in most lively dread, gets a firm foothold in London. In that case I have a notion that there will be scenes and panics. They live too well here, and have too much to make life worth clinging to—clubs, and shop fronts, and gas, and theatres, and so forth—things that they affect to despise, and whereon and whereby they live like leeches. But I have written enough. It doesn't exhaust the subject; but you won't be grateful for other epistles. De Vitre of the Poona Irregular Moguls will have it that they are a tiddyiddy people. He says that all their visible use is to produce loans for the colonies and men to be used up in developing India. I honestly believe that the average Englishman would faint if you told him it was lawful to use up human life for any purpose whatever. He believes that it has to be developed and made beautiful for the possessor, and in that belief talkatively perpetrates cruelties that would make Torquemada jump in his grave. Go to Alipur if you want to see. I am off to foreign parts—forty miles away—to catch fish for my friend the char-cat; also to shoot a little bird if I have luck.

Yours,
RUDYARD KIPLING.

II

To Lieutenant John McHail,
151st (Kumharsen) N.I.,
Hakaiti via Tharanda.

Captain Sahib Bahadur! The last Pi gives me news of your step, and I'm more pleased about it than many. You've been "cavalry quick" in your promotion. Eight years and your company! Allahu! But it must have been that long, lean horse-head of yours that looks so wise and says so little that has imposed upon the authorities. My best congratulations. Let out your belt two holes, and be happy, as I am not.

Did I tell you in my last about going to Woking in search of a grave? The dust and the grime and the grey and the sausage-shop told on my spirits to such an extent that I solemnly took a train and went grave-hunting through the Necropolis—locally called the Necrapolis. I wanted an eligible, entirely detached site in a commanding position—six by three and bricked throughout. I found it, but the only drawback was that I must go back to town to the head office to buy it. One doesn't go to town to haggle for tomb-space, so I deferred the matter and went fishing. All the same, there are very nice graves at Woking, and I shall keep my eye on one of 'em.

Since that date I seem to have been in four or five places, because there are labels on the bag. One of the places was Plymouth, where I found half a regiment at field exercises on the Hoe. They were practising the attack in three lines with the mixed rush at the end, even as it is laid down in the drill-book, and they charged subduedly across the Hoe. The people laughed. I was much more inclined to cry. Except the Major, there didn't seem to be anything more than twenty years old in the regiment; and oh! but it was pink and white and chubby and undersized—just made to die succulently of disease. I fancied that some of our battalions out with you were more or less young and exposed, but a home battalion is a crèche, and it scares one to watch it. Eminent and distinguished Generals get up after dinner—I've listened to two of 'em—and explain that though the home battalion can only be regarded as a feeder to the foreign, yet all our battalions can be regarded as efficient; and if they aren't efficient we shall find in our military reserve the nucleus—how I loath that lying word!—of the Lord knows what, but the speeches always end with allusions to the spirit of the English, their glorious past, and the certainty that when the hour of need comes the nation will "emerge victorious." If (sic) the Engineer of the Hungerford Bridge told the South-eastern Railway that because a main girder had stood for thirty years without need of renewal it was therefore sure to stand for another fifty, he would probably get the sack. Our military authorities don't get the sack. They are allowed to make speeches in public. Some day, if we live long enough, we shall see the glories of the past and the "sublime instinct of an ancient people" without one complete army corps, pitted against a few unsentimental long-range guns and some efficiently organised troops. Then the band will begin to play, and it will not play Rule Britannia until it has played some funny tunes first.

Do you remember Tighe? He was in the Deccan Lancers and retired because he got married. He is in Ireland now, and I met him the other day, idle, unhappy and dying for some work to do. Mrs. Tighe is equally miserable. She wants to go back to Poona instead of administering a big barrack of a house somewhere at the back of a bog. I quote Tighe here. He has, you may remember, a pretty tongue about him, and he was describing to me at length how a home regiment behaves when it is solemnly turned out for a week or a month training under canvas:

"About four in the mornin', me dear boy, they begin pitchin' their tents for the next day—four hours to pitch it, and the tent ropes a howlin' tangle when all's said and sworn. Then they tie their horses with strings to their big toes and go to bed in hollows and caves in the earth till the rain falls and the tents are flooded, and then, me dear boy, the men and the horses and the ropes and the vegetation of the country cuddle each other till the morning for the company's sake. And next day it all begins again. Just when they are beginning to understand how to camp they are all put back into their boxes, and half of 'em have lung disease."

But what is the use of snarling and grumbling? The matter will adjust itself later on, and the one nation on earth that talks and thinks most of the sanctity of human life will be a little astonished at the waste of life for which it will be responsible. In those days, my captain, the man who can command seasoned troops and have made the best use of those troops will be sought after and petted and will rise to honour. Remember the Hakaiti when next you measure the naked recruit.

Let us revisit calmer scenes. I've been down for three perfect days to the seaside. Don't you remember what a really fine day means? A milk-white sea, as smooth as glass, with blue-white heat haze hanging over it, one little wave talking to itself on the sand, warm shingle, four bathing machines, cliff in the background, and half the babies in Christendom paddling and yelling. It was a queer little place, just near enough to the main line of traffic to be overlooked from morning till night. There was a baby—an Ollendorfian baby—with whom I fell madly in love. She lived down at the bottom of a great white sunbonnet; talked French and English in a clear, bell-like voice, and of such I fervently hope will the Kingdom of Heaven be. When she found that my French wasn't equal to hers she condescendingly talked English and bade me build her houses of stones and draw cats for her through half the day. After I had done everything that she ordered she went off to talk to some one else. The beach belonged to that baby, and every soul on it was her servant, for I know that we rose with shouts when she paddled into three inches of water and sat down, gasping: "Mon Dieu! Je suis mort!" I know you like the little ones, so I don't apologise for yarning about them. She had a sister aged seven and one-half—a lovely child, without a scrap of self-consciousness, and enormous eyes. Here comes a real tragedy. The girl—and her name was Violet—had fallen wildly in love with a little fellow of nine. They used to walk up the single street of the village with their arms round each other's necks. Naturally, she did all the little wooings, and Hugh submitted quietly. Then devotion began to pall, and he didn't care to paddle with Violet. Hereupon, as far as I can gather, she smote him on the head and threw him against a wall. Anyhow, it was very sweet and natural, and Hugh told me about it when I came down. "She's so unrulable," he said. "I didn't hit her back, but I was very angry." Of course, Violet repented, but Hugh grew suspicious, and at the psychological moment there came down from town a destroyer of delights and a separator of companions in the shape of a tricycle. Also there were many little boys on the beach—rude, shouting, romping little chaps—who said: "Come along!" "Hullo!" and used the wicked word "beastly!" Among these Hugh became a person of importance and began to realise that he was a man who could say "beastly," and "Come on!" with the best of 'em. He preferred to run about with the little boys on wars and expeditions, and he wriggled away when Violet put her arm round his waist. Violet was hurt and angry, and I think she slapped Hugh. Relations were strained when I arrived because one morning Violet, after asking permission, invited Hugh to come to lunch. And that bad, Spanish-eyed boy deliberately filled his bucket with the cold seawater and dashed it over Violet's pink ankles. (Joking apart, this seems to be about the best way of refusing an invitation that civilisation can invent. Try it on your Colonel.) She was madly angry for a moment, and then she said: "Let me carry you up the beach, 'cause of the shingles in your toes." This was divine, but it didn't move Hugh, and Violet went off to her mother. She sat down with her chin in her hand, looking out at the sea for a long time very sorrowfully. Then she said, and it was her first experience: "I know that Hugh cares more for his horrid bicycle than he does for me, and if he said he didn't I wouldn't believe him."

Up to date Hugh has said nothing. He is running about playing with the bold, bad little boys, and Violet is sitting on a breakwater, trying to find out why things are as they are. It's a nice tale, and tales are scarce these days. Have you noticed how small and elemental is the stock of them at the world's disposal? Men foregathered at that little seaside place, and, manlike, exchanged stories. They were all the same stories. One had heard 'em in the East with Eastern variations, and in the West with Western extravagances tacked on. Only one thing seemed new, and it was merely a phrase used by a groom in speaking of an ill-conditioned horse: "No, sir; he's not ill in a manner o' speaking, but he's so to speak generally unfriendly with his innards as a usual thing."

I entrust this to you as a sacred gift. See that it takes root in the land. "Unfriendly with his innards as a usual thing." Remember. It's better than laboured explanations in the rains. And I fancy it's raw.

And now. But I had nearly forgotten. We're a nation of grumblers, and that's why other people call Anglo-Indians bores. I write feelingly because M—, just home on long leave, has for the second time sat on my devoted head for two hours simply and solely for the purpose of swearing at the Accountant-General. He has given me the whole history of his pay, prospects and promotion twice over, and in case I should misunderstand wants me to dine with him and hear it all for the third time. If M— would leave the A.-G. alone he is a delightful man, as we all know; but he's loose in London now, button-holing English friends and quoting leave and pay codes to them. He wants to see a Member of Parliament about something or other, and I believe he spends his nights rolled up in a rezai on the stairs of the India Office waiting to catch a secretary. I like the India Office. They are so beautifully casual and lazy, and their rooms look out over the Green Park, and they are never tired of admiring the view. Now and then a man comes in to report himself, and the secretaries and the under-secretaries and the chaprassies play battledore and shuttlecock with him until they are tired.

Some time since, when I was better, more serious and earnest than I am now, I preached a jehad up and down those echoing corridors, and suggested the abolition of the India Office and the purchase of a four-pound-ten American revolving bookcase to hold all the documents on India that were of public value or could be comprehended by the public. Now I am more frivolous because I am dropping gently into that grave at Woking; and yet I believe in the bookcase. India is bowed down with too much duftar as it is, and the House of Correction, Revision, Division and Supervision cannot do her much good. I saw a committee or a council file in the other day. Only one desirable tale came to me out of that office. If you've heard it before stop me. It began with a cutting from an obscure Welsh paper, I think, A man—a gardener—went mad, announced that Lord Cross was the Messiah and burned himself alive on a pile of garden refuse. That's the first part. I never could get at the second, but I am credibly informed that the work of the India Office stood still for three weeks, while the entire staff took council how to break the news to the Secretary of State. I believe it still remains unbroken.

Decidedly, leave in England is a disappointing thing. I've wandered into two stations since I wrote the last. Nothing but the labels on the bag remain—oh, and a memory of a weighing-in at an East End fishing club. That was an experience. I foregathered with a man on the top of a 'bus, and we became great friends because we both agreed that gorgetackle for pike was only permissible in very weedy streams. He repeated his views, which were my views, nearly ten times, and in the evening invited me to this weighing-in, at, we'll say, rooms of the Lea and Chertsey Piscatorial Anglers' Benevolent Brotherhood. We assembled in a room at the top of a public house, the walls ornamented with stuffed fish and water-birds, and the anglers came in by twos and threes, and I was introduced to all of 'em as "the gen'elman I met just now." This seemed to be good enough for all practical purposes. There were ten and five shilling prizes, and the affable and energetic clerk of the scales behaved as though he were weighing-in for the Lucknow races. The take of the day was one pound fifteen ounces of dace and roach, about twenty fingerlings, and the winner, who is in charge of a railway bookstall, described minutely how he had caught each fish. As a matter of fact, roach-fishing in the Lea and Thames is a fine art. Then there were drinks—modest little drinks—and they called upon me for a sentiment. You know how things go at the sergeants' messes and some of the lodges. In a moment of brilliant inspiration I gave "free fishing in the parks" and brought down the whole house. Sah! free fishing for coarse fish in the Serpentine and the Green Park water would hurt nobody and do a great deal of good to many. The stocking of the water—but what does this interest you? The Englishman moves slowly. He is just beginning to understand that it is not sufficient to set apart a certain amount of land for a lung of London and to turn people into it with "There, get along and play," unless he gives 'em something to play with. Thirty years hence he will almost allow cafés and hired bands in Hyde Park.

To return for a moment to the fish club. I got away at eleven, and in darkness and despair had to make my way west for leagues and leagues across London. I was on the Mile End Road at midnight and there lost myself, and learned something more about the policeman. He is haughty in the East and always afraid that he is being chaffed. I honestly only wanted sailing directions to get homeward. One policeman said: "Get along. You know your way as well as I do." And yet another: "You go back to the country where you comed from. You ain't doin' no good 'ere!" It was so deadly true that I couldn't answer back, and there wasn't an expensive cab handy to prove my virtue and respectability. Next time I visit the Lea and Chertsey Affabilities I'll find out something about trains. Meantime I keep holiday dolefully. There is not anybody to play with me. They have all gone away to their own places. Even the Infant, who is generally the idlest man in the world, writes me that he is helping to steer a ten-ton yacht in Scottish seas. When she heels over too much the Infant is driven to the O.P. side and she rights herself. The Infant's host says: "Isn't this bracing? Isn't this delightful?" And the Infant, who lives in dread of a chill bringing back his Indian fever, has to say "Ye-es," and pretend to despise overcoats. Wallah! This is a cheerful world.

RUDYARD KIPLING.

The Adoration of the Mage

This is a slim, thin little story, but it serves to explain a great many things. I picked it up in a four-wheeler in the company of an eminent novelist, a pink-eyed young gentleman who lived on his income, and a gentleman who knew more than he ought; and I preserved it, thinking it would serve to interest you. It may be an old story, but the G.W.K.T.H.O., whom, for the sake of brevity, we will call Captain Kydd, declared that his best friend had heard it himself. Consequently, I doubted its newness more than ever. For when a man raises his voice and vows that the incident occurred opposite his own Club window, all the listening world know that they are about to hear what is vulgarly called a cracker. This rule holds good in London as well as in Lahore. When we left the house of the highly distinguished politician who had been entertaining us, we stepped into a London Particular, which has nothing whatever to do with the story, but was interesting from the little fact that we could not see our hands before our faces. The black, brutal fog had turned each gas-jet into a pin-prick of light, visible only at six inches range. There were no houses, there were no pavements. There were no points of the compass. There were only the eminent novelist, the young gentleman with the pink eyes. Captain Kydd and myself, holding each other's shoulders in the gloom of Tophet. Then the eminent novelist delivered himself of an epigram.

"Let's go home," said he.

"Let us try," said Captain Kydd, and incontinently fell down an area into somebody's kitchen yard and disappeared into chaos. When he had climbed out again we heard a something on wheels swearing even worse than Captain Kydd was, all among the railings of a square. So .we shouted, and presently a four-wheeler drove gracefully on to the pavement.

"I'm trying to get 'ome," said the cabby. "But if you gents make it worth while . . . though heaven knows 'ow we ever shall. Guess 'arf a crown apiece might . . . and any'ow I won't promise anywheres in particular."

The cabby kept his word nobly. He did not find anywheres in particular, but he found several places. First he discovered a pavement kerb and drove pressing his wheel against it till we came to a lamp-post, and that we hit grievously. Then he came to what ought to have been a corner, but was a 'bus, and we embraced the thing amid terrific language. Then he sailed out into nothing at all—blank fog—and there he commended himself to heaven and his horse to the other place, while the eminent novelist put his head out of the window and gave directions. I begin to understand now why the eminent novelist's villains are so lifelike and his plots so obscure. He has a marvellous breadth of speech, but no ingenuity in directing the course of events. We drove into the island of refuge near the Brompton Oratory just when he was telling the cabby to be sure and avoid the Regents' Park Canal.

Then we began to talk about the weather and Mister Gladstone. If an Englishman is unhappy he always talks about Mister Gladstone in terms of reproof. The eminent novelist was a socialistic-Neo-Plastic-Unionistic-Demagoglot Radical of the Extreme Left, and that is the latest novelty of the thing yet invented. He withdrew his head to answer Captain Kydd's arguments, which were forcible. "Well, you'll admit he's all sorts of a madman," said Captain Kydd sweetly. "He's a saint," said the eminent novelist, "and he moves in an atmosphere that you and those like you cannot breathe."

"Yes, I always said it was a pretty thick fog. Now I know it's as thick as this one. I say, we're on the pavement again; we shall be in a shop in a minute," said Captain Kydd.

But I wanted to see the eminent novelist fight, so I reintroduced Mister Gladstone while the cab crawled up a wall.

"It's not exactly a wholesome atmosphere," said Captain Kydd when the novelist had finished speaking. "That reminds me of a story—perfectly true story. In the old days, before he went off his chump—"

"Yah-h-h!" said the eminent novelist, wrapping himself in his Inverness.

"—went off his nut, he used to consort a good deal with his friends on his own side—visit 'em, y' know, and deliver addresses out of their own bedroom windows, and steal their postcards, and generally be friendly. Well, one man he stayed with had a house, a country house, y' know, and in the garden there was a path which was supposed to divide Kent and Surrey or some counties. They led the old man forth for his walk, y' know, and followed him in gangs to hear that the weather was fine, and of course his host pointed out the path, the old man took in the situation, and put one I daresay they had strewn rose-leaves on it, or spread it with homespun trousers. Anyhow, one leg on one side of the path and the other on the other, and with one of those wonderful flashes of humour that come to him when he chooses to frisk among his friends, he said: 'Now I am in Kent and in Surrey at the same time.'"

Captain Kydd ceased speaking as the cab tried to force a way into the South Kensington Museum.

"Well, what's there in that?" said the eminent novelist.

"Oh, nothing much. Let's see how it goes afterwards. Mrs. Gladstone, who was close behind him, turned round and whispered to the hostess in an ecstatic shriek: 'Oh, Mrs. Whateverhemamewas, you will plant a tree there, won't you?' "

"By Jove!" said the young gentleman with the pink eyes.

"I don't believe it," said the eminent novelist.

I said nothing, but it seemed very likely. Captain Kydd laughed: "Well, I don't consider that sort of atmosphere exactly wholesome, y' know."

And when the cab had landed us in the drinking-fountain in High Street, Kensington, and the horse fell down, and the cabby collected our half-crowns and gave us his beery blessing, and I had to grope my way home on foot, it occurred to me that perhaps you might be interested in that anecdote. As I have said, it explains a great deal more than appears at first sight.

A Death in the Camp

Two awful catastrophes have occurred. One Englishman in London is dead, and I have scandalised about twenty of his nearest and dearest friends. He was a man nearly seventy years old, engaged in the business of an architect, and immensely respected. That was all I knew about him till I began to circulate among his friends in these parts, trying to cheer them up and make them forget the fog.

"Hush!" said a man and his wife. "Don't you know he died yesterday of a sudden attack of pneumonia? Isn't it shocking?"

"Yes," said I vaguely. "Aw'fly shocking. Has he left his wife provided for?"

"Oh, he's very well off indeed, and his wife is quite old. But just think—it was only in the next street it happened!" Then I saw that their grief was not for Strangeways, deceased, but for themselves.

"How old was he?" I said.

"Nearly seventy, or maybe a little over."

"About time for a man to rationally expect such a thing as death," I thought, and went away to another house, where a young married couple lived.

"Isn't it perfectly ghastly?" said the wife. "Mr. Strangeways died last night."

"So I heard," said I. "Well, he had lived his life."

"Yes, but it was such a shockingly short illness. Why, only three weeks ago he was walking about the street." And she looked nervously at her husband, as though she expected him to give up the ghost at any minute.

Then I gathered, with the knowledge of the length of his sickness, that her grief was not for the late Mr. Strangeways, and went away thinking over men and women I had known who would have given a thousand years in Purgatory for even a week wherein to arrange their affairs, and who were anything but well off.

I passed on to a third house full of children, and the shadow of death hung over their heads, for father and mother were talking of Mr. Strangeway's "end." "Most shocking," said they. "It seems that his wife was in the next room when he was dying, and his only son called her, so she just had time to take him in her arms before he died. He was unconscious at the last. Wasn't it awful?"

When I went away from that house I thought of men and women without a week wherein to arrange their affairs, and without any money, who were anything but unconscious at the last, and who would have given a thousand years in Purgatory for one glimpse at their mothers, their wives or their husbands. I reflected how these people died tended by hirelings and strangers, and I was not in the least ashamed to say that I laughed over Mr. Strangeways' death as I entered the house of a brother in his craft.

"Heard of Strangeways' death?" said he. "Most hideous thing. Why, he had only a few days before got news of his designs being accepted by the Burgoyne Cathedral. If he had lived he would have been working out the details now—with me." And I saw that this man's fear also was not on account of Mr. Strangeways. And I thought of men and women who had died in the midst of wrecked work; then I sought a company of young men and heard them talk of the dead. "That's the second death among people I know within the year," said one. "Yes, the second death," said another.

I smiled a very large smile.

"And you know," said a third, who was the oldest of the party, "they've opened the new road by the head of Tresillion Road, and the wind blows straight across that level square from the Parks. Everything is changing about us."

"He was an old man," I said.

"Ye-es. More than middle-aged," said they.

"And he outlived his reputation?"

"Oh, no, or how would he have taken the designs for the Burgoyne Cathedral? Why, the very day he died . . ."

"Yes," said I. "He died at the end of a completed work—his design finished, his prize awarded?"

"Yes; but he didn't live to . . ."

"And his illness lasted seventeen days, of twenty-four hours each?"

"Yes."

"And he was tended by his own kith and kin, dying with his head on his wife's breast, his hand in his only son's hand, without any thought of their possible poverty to vex him. Are these things so?"

"Ye-es," said they. "Wasn't it shocking?"

"Shocking?" I said. "Get out of this place. Go forth, run about and see what death really means. You have described such dying as a god might envy and a king might pay half his ransom to make certain of. Wait till you have seen men—strong men of thirty-five, with little children, die at two days' notice, penniless and alone, and seen it not once, but twenty times; wait till you have seen the young girl die within a fortnight of the wedding; or the lover within three days of his marriage; or the mother—sixty little minutes—before her son can come to her side; wait till you hesitate before handling your daily newspaper for fear of reading of the death of some young man that you have dined with, drank with, shot with, lent money to and borrowed money from, and tested to the uttermost—till you dare not hope for the death of an old man, but, when you are strongest, count up the tale of your acquaintances and friends, wondering how many will be alive six months hence. Wait till you have heard men calling in the death hour on kin that cannot come; till you have dined with a man one night and seen him buried on the next. Then you can begin to whimper about loneliness and change and desolation." Here I foamed at the mouth.

"And do you mean to say," drawled a young gentleman, "that there is any society in which that sort of holocaust goes on?"

"I do," said I. "It's not society; it's Life," And they laughed.

But this is the old tale of Pharaoh's chariot-wheel and flying-fish.

If I tell them yarns, they say: "How true! How true!" If I try to present the truth, they say: "What superb imagination!"

"But you understand, don't you?'

A Really Good Time

There are times when one wants to get into pyjamas and stretch and loll, and explain things generally. This is one of those times. It is impossible to stand at ease in London, and the inhabitants are so abominably egotistical that one cannot shout "I, I, I" for two minutes without another man joining in with "Me, too!" Which things are an allegory.

The amusement began with a gentleman of infinite erudition offering to publish my autobiography. I was to write a string of legends—he would publish them; and would I forward a cheque for five guineas "to cover incidental expenses?" To him I explained that I wanted five guinea cheques myself very much indeed, and that, emboldened by his letter, which gave me a very fair insight into his character, I was even then maturing his autobiography, which I hoped to publish before long with illustrations, and would he forward a cheque for five guineas "to cover incidental expenses?" This brought me an eight-page compilation of contumely. He was grieved to find that he had been mistaken in my character, which he had believed was, at least, elevated. He begged me to remember that the first letter had been written in the strictest confidence, and that if I notated one tittle of the said "repository" he would unkennel the bloodhounds of the law and hunt me down. An autobiography on the lines that I had "so flippantly proposed" was libel without benefit of authorship, and I had better lend him two guineas—I.O.U. enclosed—to salve his lacerated feelings. I replied that I had his autobiography by me in manuscript, and would post it to his address, V.P.P., two guineas and one-half. He evidently knew nothing about the V.P.P., and the correspondence stopped. It is really very hard for an Anglo-Indian to get along in London. Besides, my autobiography is not a thing I should care to make public before extensive Bowdlerisation.

These things, however, only led up to much worse. I dare not grin over them unless I step aside Eastward. I wrote stories, all about little pieces of India, carefully arranged and expurgated for the English public. Then various people began to write about them. One gentleman pointed out that I had taken "the well-worn themes of passion, love, despair and fate," and, thanks to the "singular fascination" of my style had "wrought them into new and glowing fabricks instinct with the eternal vitality of the East." For three days after this chit I was almost too proud to speak to the housemaid with the fan-teeth (there is a story about her that I will tell another time). On the fourth day another gentleman made clear that that beautiful style was "tortuous, elaborated and inept," and it was only on account of the "newness of the subjects handled so crabbedly" that I "arrested the attention of the public for a day." Then I wept before the housemaid, and she called me a "real gentleman" because I gave her a shilling.

Then I tried an all-round cannon—published one thing under one name and another under another, and sat still to watch. A gentleman, who also speaks with authority on Literature and Art, came to me and said: "I don't deny that there is a great deal of clever and superficial fooling in that last thing of yours in the—I've forgotten what it was called—but do you yourself think that you have that curious, subtle grip on and instinct of matters Oriental that that other man shows in his study of native life?" And he mentioned the name of my Other Self. I bowed my head, and my shoulders shook with repentance and grief. "No," said I. "It's so true," said he. "Yes," said I. "So feeling," said he. "Indeed it is," said I. "Such honest work, too!" said he. "Oh, awful!" said I. "Think it over," said he, "and try to follow his path." "I will," said I. And when he left I danced sarabands with the housemaid of the fan-teeth till she wanted to know whether I had bought "spirruts."

Then another man came along and sat on my sofa and hailed me as a brother. "And I know that we are kindred souls," said he, "because I feel sure that you have evolved all the dreamy mystery and curious brutality of the British soldier from the pure realm of fancy." "I did," I said. "If you went into a barrack-room you would see at once." "Faugh!" said he. "What have we to do with barrack-rooms? The pure air of fancy feeds us both; keep to that. If you are trammelled by the bitter, bornée truth, you are lost. You die the death of Zola. Invention is the only test of creation." "Of course," said I. "Zola's a bold, bad man. Not a patch on you," I hadn't caught his name, but I fancied that would prevent him flinging himself about on my sofa, which is a cheap one. "I don't say that altogether," he said. "He has his strong points. But he is deficient in imaginative constructiveness. You, I see from what you have said, will belong to the Neo-Gynekalistic school." I knew "Gyne" meant something about cow-killing, and was prepared to hedge when he said good-bye, and wrote an article about my ways and works, which brought another man to my door spouting foam.

"Great Landor's ghost!" he said. "What under the stars has possessed you to join the Gynekalistic lot?" "I haven't," I said. "I believe in municipal regulation of slaughterhouses, if there is a strong Deputy Commissioner to control the Muhanunadan butchers, especially in the hot weather, but . . ." "This is madness," said he. "Your reputation is at stake. You must make it clear to the world that you have nothing whatever to do with the flatulent, imballasted fiction of . . ." "Do you suppose the world cares a tuppeny dam?" said I.

Then he raged afresh, and left me, pointing out that the Gynewallahs wrote about nothing but women—which seems rather an unlimited subject—and that I would die the death of a French author whose name I have forgotten. But it wasn't Zola this time.

I asked the housemaid what in the world the Gynekalisthenics were. "La, sir," said she, "it's only their way of being rude. That fat gentleman with the long hair tried to kiss me when I opened the door. I slapped his fat chops for him."

Now the crisis is at its height. All the entire round world, composed, as far as I can learn, of the Gynekalistic and the anti-Gynekalistic man, and two or three loafers, are trying to find out to what school I rightly belong. They seem to use what they are pleased to call my reputation as a bolster through which to stab at the foe. One gentleman is proving that I am a bit of a blackguard, probably reduced from the ranks, rather an impostor, and a considerable amount of plagiarist. The other man denies the reduction from the ranks, withholds judgment about the plagiarism, but would like, in the interest of the public—who are at present exclusively occupied with Barnum—to prove it true, and is convinced that my style is "hermaphroditic." I have all the money on the first man. He is on the eve of discovering that I stole a dead Tommy's diary just before I was drummed out of the service for desertion, and have lived on the proceeds ever since. "Do yew know," as the Private Secretary said at Simla this year, "it's remarkably hard for an Anglo-Indian to get along in England."

Shakl hai lekin ukl nahin hai!

It makes me blush pink all over to think about it, but, none the less, I have brought the tale to you, confident that you will understand. An invitation to tea arrived at my address. The English are very peculiar people about their tea. They don't seem to understand that it is a function at which any one who is passing down the Mall may present himself. They issue formal cards—just as if tea-drinking were like dancing. My invitation said that I was to tea from 4:30 till 6 p.m., and there was never a word of lawn-tennis on the whole of the card. I knew the English were heavy eaters, but this amazed me. "What in the wide world," thought I, "will they find to do for an hour and a half? Perhaps they'll play games, as it's near Christmas time. They can't sit out in the verandah, and chabutras are impossible,"

Wherefore I went to this house prepared for anything. There was a fine show of damp wraps in the hall, and a cheerful babble of voices from the other side of the drawing-room door. The hostess ran at me, vehemently shouting: "Oh, I am so glad you have come. We were all talking about you." As the room was entirely filled with strangers, chiefly female, I reflected that they couldn't have said anything very bad. Then I was introduced to everybody, and some of the people were talking in couples, and didn't want to be interrupted in the least, and some were behind settees, and some were in difficulty with their tea-cups, and one and all had exactly the same name. That is the worst of a lisping hostess.

Almost before I had dropped the last limp hand, a burly ruffian, with a beard, rumbled in my ear: "I trust you were satisfied with my estimate of your powers in last week's Concertina?"

Now I don't see the Concertina because it's too expensive, but I murmured: "Immense! immense! Most gratifying. Totally undeserved." And the ruffian said: "In a measure, yes. Not wholly. I flatter myself that—"

"Oh, not in the least," said I. "No sugar, thanks." This to the hostess, who was waving Sally Lunns under my nose. A female, who could not have been less than seven feet high, came on, half speed ahead, through the fog of the tea-steam, and docked herself on the sofa just like an Inman liner.

"Have you ever considered," said she, "the enormous moral responsibility that rests in the hands of one who has the gift of literary expression? In my own case—but you surely know my collaborator."

A much huger woman arrived, cast anchor, and docked herself on the other side of the sofa. She was the collaborator. Together they confided to me that they were desperately in earnest about the amelioration of something or other. Their collective grievance against me was that I was not in earnest.

"We have studied your works—all," said the five-thousand-ton four-master, "and we cannot believe that you are in earnest," "Oh, no," I said hastily, "I never was." Then I saw that that was the wrong thing to say, for the eight-thousand-ton palace Cunarder signalled to the sister ship, saying; "You see, my estimate was correct."

"Now, my complaint against him is that he is too savagely farouche" said a weedy young gentleman with tow hair, who ate Sally Lunns like a workhouse orphan. "Faroucherie in his age is a fatal mistake."

I reflected a moment on the possibility of getting that young gentleman out into a large and dusty maidan and gently chukkering him before chota hazri. He looked too sleek to me as he then stood. But I said nothing, because a tiny-tiny woman with beady-black eyes shrilled: "I disagree with you entirely. He is too much bound by the tradition of the commonplace. I have seen in his later work signs that he is afraid of his public. You must never be afraid of your public."

Then they began to discuss me as though I were dead and buried under the hearth-rug, and they talked of "tones" and "notes" and lights" and "shades" and tendencies.

"And which of us do you think is correct in her estimate of your character?" said the tiny-tiny woman when they had made me out (a) a giddy Lothario; (b) a savage; (c) a pre-Rafaelite angel; (d) co-equal and co-eternal with half a dozen gentlemen whose names I had never heard; (e) flippant; (f) penetrated with pathos; (g) an open atheist; (h) a young man of the Roman Catholic faith with a mission in life.

I smiled idiotically, and said I really didn't know.

Then a man entered whom I knew, and I fled to him for comfort. "Have I missed the fun?" he asked with a twinkle in his eye.

I explained, snorting, what had befallen.

"Ay," said he quietly, "you didn't go the right way to work. You should have stood on the hearth-rug and fired off epigrams. That's what I did after I had written Down in the Doldrums, and was fed with crumpets in consequence."

A woman plumped down by my side and twisted her hands into knots, and hung her eyes over her cheek-bones, I thought it was too many muffins, till she said: "Tell me, oh, tell me, was such-and-such in such a one of your books—was he real? Was he quite real? Oh, how lovely! How sweet! How precious!" She alluded to that drunken ruffian Mulvaney, who would have driven her into fits had he ever set foot on her doorstep in the flesh. I caught the half of a wink in my friend's eye as he removed himself and left me alone to tell fibs about the evolution of Private Mulvaney. I said anything that came uppermost, and my answers grew so wild that the woman departed.

Then I heard the hostess whispering to a girl, a nice, round, healthy English maiden. "Go and talk to him," she said. "Talk to him about his books."

I gritted my teeth, and waited till the maiden was close at hand and about to begin. There was a lovely young man at the end of the room sucking a stick, and I felt sure that the maiden would much have preferred talking to him. She smiled prefatorily.

"It's hot here," I said; "let's go over to the window"; and I plumped down on a three-seated settee, with my back to the young man, leaving only one place for the maiden. I was right. I signalled up the man who had written Down in the Doldrums, and talked to him as fast as I knew how. When he had to go, and the young man with him, the maiden became enthusiastic, not to say gushing. But I knew that those compliments were for value received. Then she explained that she was going out to India to stay with her married aunt, wherefore she became as a sister unto me on the spot. Her mamma did not seem to know much about Indian outfits, and I waxed eloquent on the subject.

"It's all nonsense," I said, "to fill your boxes with things that can be made just as well in the country. What you want are walking-dresses and dinner-dresses as good as ever you can get, and gloves tinned up, and odds and ends of things generally. All the rest, unless you're extravagant, the dharzee can make in the verandah. Take underclothing, for instance." I was conscious that my loud and cheerful voice was ploughing through one of those ghostly silences that sometimes fall upon a company. The English only wear their outsides in company. They have nothing to do with underclothing. I could feel that without being told. So the silence cut short the one matter in which I could really have been of use.

On the pavement my friend who wrote Down in the Doldrums was waiting to walk home with me. "What in the world does it all mean?" I said. "Nothing," said he. "You've been asked there as a small deputy lion to roar in place of a much bigger man. You growled, though."

"I should have done much worse if I'd known," I grunted. "Ah," said he, "you haven't arrived at the real fun of the show. Wait till they've made you jump through hoops and your turn's over, and you can sit on a sofa and watch the new men being brought up and put through their paces. You've nothing like that in India. How do you manage your parties?"

And I thought of smooth-cut lawns in the gloaming, and tables spread under mighty trees, and men and women, all intimately acquainted with each other, strolling about in the lightest of raiment, and the old dowagers criticising the badminton, and the young men in riding-boots making rude remarks about the claret cup, and the host circulating through the mob and saying: "Hah, Piggy," or Bobby or Flatnose, as the nickname might be, "have another peg," and the hostess soothing the bashful youngsters and talking khitmatgars with the Judge's wife, and the last new bride hanging on her husband's arm and saying: "Isn't it almost time to go home, Dicky, dear?" and the little fat owls chuckling in the bougainvilleas and the horses stamping and squealing in the carriage-drive, and everybody saying the most awful things about everybody else, but prepared to do anything for anybody else just the same, and I gulped a great gulp of sorrow and homesickness.

"You wouldn't understand," said I to my friend lets go to a pothouse where cabbies call and drink something.

London in the Fog

"Curiouser and curiouser," as Alice in Wonderland said when she found her neck beginning to grow. Each day under the smoke brings me new and generally unpleasant discoveries. The latest are most on my mind. I hasten to transfer them to yours.

At first, and several times afterwards, I very greatly desired to talk to a thirteen-two subaltern—not because he or I would have anything valuable to say to each other, but just because he was a subaltern. I wanted to know all about that evergreen polo-pony that "can turn on a sixpence," and the second-hand charger that, by a series of perfectly unprecedented misfortunes, just failed to win the Calcutta Derby. Then, too, I wished to hear of many old friends across the sea, and who had got his company, and why and where the new Generals were going next cold weather, and how the Commander-in-Chief had been enlivening the Simla season. So I looked east and west, and north and south, but never a thirteen-two subaltern broke through the fog; except once—and he had grown a fifteen-one cot down, and wore a tall hat and frock coat, and was begging for coppers from the Horse-Guards. By the way, if you stand long enough between the mounted sentries—the men who look like reflectors stolen from Christmas trees—you will presently meet every human being you ever knew in India. When I am not happy—that is to say, once a day—I run off and play on the pavement in front of the Horse-Guards, and watch the expressions on the gentlemen's faces as they come out. But this is a digression.

After some days—I grew lonelier and lonelier every hour—I went away to the other end of the town, and catching a friend, said: "Lend me a man—a young man—to play with. I don't feel happy. I want rousing. I have liver." And the friend said: "Ah, yes, of course. What you want is congenial society, something that will stir you up—a fellow-mind. Now let me introduce you to a thoroughly nice young man. He's by way of being an ardent Neo-Alexandrine, and has written some charming papers on the 'Ethics of the Wood Pavement.'" Concealing my almost visible rapture, I murmured "Oh, bliss!" as they used to say at the Gaiety, and extended the hand of friendship to a young gentleman attired after the fashion of the Neo-Alexandrines, who appear to be a sub-caste of social priests. His hand was a limp hand, his face was very smooth because he had not yet had time to grow any hair, and he wore a cloak like a policeman's cloak, but much more so. On his finger was a cameo-ring about three inches wide, and round his neck, the weather being warm, was a fawn, olive and dead-leaf comforter of soft silk—the sort of thing any right-minded man would give to his mother or his sister without being asked.

We looked at each other cautiously for some minutes. Then he said: "What do you think of the result of the Brighton election?" "Beautiful, beautiful," I said, watching his eye, which saddened, "One of the worst—that is, entirely the most absurd reductio ad absurdum of the principle of the narrow and narrow-minded majority imposing a will which is necessarily incult on a minority ammated by . . . " I forget exactly what he said they were animated by, but it was something very fine,

"When I was at Oxford," he said, "Haward of Exeter"—he spoke as one speaks of Smith of Asia—"always inculcated at the Union—By the way, you do not know, I suppose, anything of the life at Oxford?" "No," I said, anxious to propitiate, "but I remember some boys once who seduced an ekka and a pony into a Major's tent at a camp of exercise, laced up the door, and let the Major fight it out with the horse." I told that little incident in my best style, and was three parts through it before I discovered that he was looking pained and shocked.

"That—ah—was not the side of Oxford that I had in mind when I was saying that Haward of Exeter—" And he explained all about Mr. Haward, who appeared to be a young gentleman, rising twenty-three, of wonderful mental attainments, and as pernicious a prig as I ever dreamed about. Mr. Haward had schemes for the better management of creation; my friend told me them all—social, political and economical.

Then, just as I was feeling faint and very much in need of a drink, he launched without warning upon the boundless seas of literature. He wished to know whether I had read the works of Messrs. Guy de Maupassant, Paul Bourget and Pierre Loti. This in the tone of a teacher of Euclid. I replied that all my French was confined to the Vie Parisienne and translations of Zola's novels with illustrations. Here we parted. London is very large, and I do not think we shall meet any more.

I thanked our Mutual Friend for his kindness, and asked for another young man to play with. This gentleman was even younger than the last, but quite as cocksure. He told me in the course of half a cigar that only men of mediocre calibre went into the army, which was a brutalising profession; that he suffered from nerves, and "an uncontrollable desire to walk up and down the room and sob" (that was too many cigarettes), and that he had never set foot out of England, but knew all about the world from his own theories. Thought Dickens coarse; Scott jingling and meretricious; and had not by any chance read the novels of Messrs. Guy de Maupassant, Paul Bourget and Pierre Loti.

Him I left quickly, but sorry that he could not do a six weeks' training with a Middlesex militia regiment, where he would really get something to sob for. The novel business interested me. I perceived that it was a fashion, like his tie and his collars, and I wanted to work it to the fountain-head. To this end I procured the whole Shibboleth from Guy de Maupassant even unto Pierre Loti by way of Bourget. Unwholesome was a mild term for these interesting books, which the young men assured me that they read for style. When a fat Major makes that remark in an Indian Club, everybody hoots and laughs. But you must not laugh overseas, especially at young gentlemen who have been to Oxford and listened to Mr. Haward of Exeter.

Then I was introduced to another young man who said he belonged to a movement called Toynbee Hall, where, I gathered, young gentlemen took an indecent interest in the affairs of another caste, whom, with rare tact, they called "the poor," and told them generally how to order their lives. Such was the manner and general aggressiveness of this third young gentleman, that if he had told me that coats were generally worn and good for the protection of the body, I should have paraded Bond Street in my shirt. What the poor thought of him I could not tell, but there is no room for it in this letter. He said that there was going to be an upheaval of the classes—the English are very funny about their castes. They don't know how to handle them one little bit, and never allow them to draw water or build huts in peace—and the entire social fabric was about to be remodelled on his recommendations, and the world would be generally altered past recognition. No, he had never seen anything of the world, but close acquaintance with authorities had enabled him to form dispassionate judgments on the subjects, and had I, by any chance, read the novels of Guy de Maupassant, Pierre Loti and Paul Bourget?

It was a mean thing to do, but I couldn't help it. I had read 'em. I put him on, so to speak, far back in Paul Bourget, who is a genial sort of writer. I pinned him to one book. He could not escape from Paul Bourget. He was fed with it till he confessed—and he had been quite ready to point out its beauties— that we could not take much interest in the theories put forward in that particular book. Then I said: "Get a dictionary and read him," which severed our budding friendship.

Thereafter I sought our Mutual Friend and walked up and down his room sobbing, or words to that effect. "Good gracious!" said my friend. "Is that what's troubling you? Now, I hold the ravaging rights over half a dozen fields and a bit of a wood. You can pot rabbits there in the evenings sometimes, and anyway you get exercise. Come along."

So I went. I have not yet killed anything, but it seems wasteful to drive good powder and shot after poor little bunnies when there are so many other things in the world that would be better for an ounce and a half of number five at sixty yards—not enough to disable, but just sufficient to sting, and be pricked out with a penknife.

I should like to wield that penknife.

Whether Macdougal or Macdoodle be his name, the principle remains the same, as Mrs. Nickleby said. The gentleman appeared to hold authority in London, and by virtue of his position preached or ordained that music-halls were vulgar, if not improper. Subsequently, I gathered that the gentleman was inciting his associates to shut up certain music-halls on the ground of the vulgarity afore-said, and I saw with my own eyes that unhappy little managers were putting notices into the comers of their programmes begging the audience to report each and every impropriety. That was pitiful, but it excited my interest.

Now, to the upright and impartial mind—which is mine—all the diversions of Heathendom—which is the British—are of equal ethnological value. And it is true that some human beings can be more vulgar in the act of discussing etchings, editions of luxury, or their own emotions, than other human beings employed in swearing at each other across the street. Therefore, following a chain of thought which does not matter, I visited very many theatres whose licenses had never been interfered with. There I discovered men and women who lived and moved and behaved according to rules which in no sort regulate human life, by tradition dead and done with, and after the customs of the more immoral ancients and Barnum. At one place the lodging-house servant was an angel, and her mother a Madonna; at a second they sounded the loud timbrel o'er a whirl of bloody axes, mobs, and brown-paper castles, and said it was not a pantomime, but Art; at a third everybody grew fabulously rich and fabulously poor every twenty minutes, which was confusing; at a fourth they discussed the Nudities and Lewdities in false-palate voices supposed to belong to the aristocracy and that tasted copper in the mouth; at a fifth they merely climbed up walls and threw furniture at each other, which is notoriously the custom of spinsters and small parsons. Next morning the papers would write about the progress of the modem drama (that was the silver paper pantomime) , and "graphic presentment of the realities of our highly complex civilisation." That was the angel housemaid. By the way, when an Englishman has been doing anything more than unusually Pagan, he generally consoles himself with "over-civilisation." It's the "martyr-to-nerves-dear" note in his equipment.

I went to the music-halls—the less frequented ones—and they were almost as dull as the plays, but they introduced me to several elementary truths. Ladies and gentlemen in eccentric, but not altogether unightly, costumes told me (a) that if I got drunk I should have a head next morning, and perhaps be fined by the magistrate; (b) that if I flirted promiscuously I should probably get into trouble; (c) that I had better tell my wife everything and be good to her, or she would be sure to find out for herself and be very bad to me; (d) that I should never lend money; or (e) fight with a stranger whose form I did not know. My friends (if I may be permitted to so call them) illustrated these facts with personal reminiscences and drove them home with kicks and prancings. At intervals circular ladies in pale pink and white would low to their audience to the effect that there was nothing half so sweet in life as "Love's Young Dream," and the billycock hats would look at the four-and-elevenpenny bonnets, and they saw that it was good and clasped hands on the strength of it. Then other ladies with shorter skirts would explain that when their husbands

Stagger home tight about two,
An' can't light the candle,
We taik the broom 'andle
An' show 'em what women can do."

Naturally, the billycocks, seeing what might befall, thought things over again, and you heard the bonnets murmuring softly under the clink of the lager-glasses: "Not me. Bill. Not me!" Now these things are basic and basaltic truths. Anybody can understand them. They are as old as Time. Perhaps the expression was occasionally what might be called coarse, but beer is beer, and best in a pewter, though you can, if you please, drink it from Venetian glass and call it something else. The halls give wisdom and not too lively entertainment for sixpence—ticket good for four pen'orth of refreshments, chiefly inky porter—and the people who listen are respectable folk living very grey skys who derive all the light side of their life, the food for their imagination and the crystallised expression of their views on Fate and Nemesis, from the affable ladies and gentlemen singers. They require a few green and gold maidens in short skirts to kick before them. Herein they are no better and no worse than folk who require fifty girls very much undressed, and a setting of music, or pictures that won't let themselves be seen on account of their age and varnish, or statues and coins. All animals like salt, but some prefer rock-salt, red or black in lumps. But this is a digression.

Out of my many visits to the hall—I chose one hall, you understand, and frequented it till I could tell the mood it was in before I had passed the ticket-poll—was born the Great Idea. I served it as a slave for seven days. Thought was not sufficient; experience was necessary. I patrolled Westminster, Blackfriars, Lambeth, the Old Kent Road, and many, many more miles of pitiless pavement to make sure of my subject. At even I drank my lager among the billycocks, and lost my heart to a bonnet. Goethe and Shakespeare were my precedents. I sympathised with them acutely, but I got my Message. A chance-caught refrain of a song which I understand is protected—to its maker I convey my most grateful acknowledgments—gave me what I sought. The rest was made up of four elementary truths, some humour, and, though I say it who should leave it to the press, pathos deep and genuine. I spent a penny on a paper which introduced me to a Great and Only who "wanted new songs." The people desired them really. He was their ambassador, and taught me a great deal about the property-right in songs, concluding with a practical illustration, for he said my verses were just the thing and annexed them. It was long before he could hit on the step-dance which exactly elucidated the spirit of the text, and longer before he could jingle a pair of huge brass spurs as a dancing-girl jingles her anklets. That was my notion, and a good one.

The Great and Only possessed a voice like a bull, and nightly roared to the people at the heels of one who was winning triple encores with a priceless ballad beginning deep down in the bass: "We was shopmates—boozin' shopmates." I feared that song as Rachel feared Ristori. A greater than I had written it. It was a grim tragedy, lighted with lucid humour, wedded to music that maddened. But my "Great and Only" had faith in me, and I—I clung to the Great Heart of the People—my people—four hxmdred "when it's all full, sir." I had not studied them for nothing. I must reserve the description of my triumph for another "Turnover."

There was no portent in the sky on the night of my triumph. A barrowful of onions, indeed, upset itself at the door, but that was a coincidence. The hall was crammed with billycocks waiting for "We was shopmates." The great heart beat healthily. I went to my beer the equal of Shakespeare and Moliere at the wings in a first night. What would my public say? Could anything live after the abandon of "We was shopmates"? What if the redcoats did not muster in their usual strength. O my friends, never in your songs and dramas forget the redcoat. He has sympathy and enormous boots.

I believed in the redcoat; in the great heart of the people: above all in myself. The conductor, who advertised that he "doctored bad songs," had devised a pleasant little lilting air for my needs, but it struck me as weak and thin after the thunderous surge of the "Shopmates." I glanced at the gallery—the redcoats were there. The fiddle-bows creaked, and, with a jingle of brazen spurs, a forage-cap over his left eye, my Great and Only began to "chuck it off his chest." Thus:

"At the back o' the Knightsbridge Barricks,
When the fog was a-gatherin' dim,
The Lifeguard talked to the Undercook,
An' the girl she talked to 'im."

"Twiddle - iddle - iddle'lum'tum-tum!" said the violins.

"Ling - a-ling-a-ling-a-ling-ting-ling!" said the spurs of the Great and Only, and through the roar in my ears I fancied I could catch a responsive hoof-beat in the gallery. The next four lines held the house to attention. Then came the chorus and the borrowed refrain. It took—it went home with a crisp click. My Great and Only saw his chance. Superbly waving his hand to embrace the whole audience, he invited them to join him in:

"You may make a mistake when you're mashing a tart.
But you'll learn to be wise when you're older,
And don't try for things that are out of your reach,
And that's what the girl told the soldier, soldier, soldier.
And that's what the girl told the soldier."

I thought the gallery would never let go of the long-drawn howl on "soldier." They clung to it as ringers to the kicking bell-rope. Then I envied no one—not even Shakespeare. I had my house hooked—gaffed under the gills, netted, speared, shot behind the shoulder—anything you please. That was pure joy! With each verse the chorus grew louder, and when my Great and Only had bellowed his way to the fall of the Lifeguard and the happy lot of the Undercook, the gallery rocked again, the reserved stalls shouted, and the pewters twinkled like the legs of the demented ballet-girls. The conductor waved the now frenzied orchestra to softer Lydian strains. My Great and Only warbled piano:

"At the back o' Knightsbridge Barricks,
When the fog's a-gatherin' dim.
The Lifeguard waits for the Undercook,
But she won't wait for 'im."

"Ta-ra-rara-rara-ra-ra-rah!" rang a horn clear and fresh as a sword-cut. 'Twas the apotheosis of virtue.

"She's married a man in the poultry line
That lives at 'Ighgate 'Ill,
An' the Lifeguard walks with the 'ousemaid now,
An' (awful pause) she can't foot the bill r

Who shall tell the springs that move masses? I had builded better than I knew. Followed yells, shrieks and wildest applause. Then, as a wave gathers to the curl-over, singer and sung to fill their chests and heave the chorus through the quivering roof—alto, horns, basses drowned, and lost in the flood—to the beach-like boom of beating feet:

"Oh, think o' my song when you're gowin' it strong
An' your boots is too little to 'old yer;
An' don't try for things that is out of your reach.
An' that's what the girl told the soldier, soldier, so-holdier!"

Ow! Hi! Yi! Wha-hup! Phew! Whew! Pwhit! Bang! Wang! Crr-rash! There was ample time for variations as the horns uplifted themselves and ere the held voices came down in the foam of sound—

"That's what the girl told the soldier."

Providence has sent me several joys, and I have helped myself to others, but that night, as I looked across the sea of tossing billycocks and rocking bonnets, my work, as I heard them give tongue, not once, but four times—their eyes sparkling, their mouths twisted with the taste of pleasure—I felt that I had secured Perfect Felicity. I am become greater than Shakespeare. I may even write plays for the Lyceum, but I never can recapture that first fine rapture that followed the Upheaval of the Anglo-Saxon four hundred of him and her. They do not call for authors on these occasions, But I desired no need of public recognition. I was placidly happy. The chorus bubbled up again and again throughout the evening, and a redcoat in the gallery insisted on singing solos about "a swine in the poultry line," whereas I had written "man," and the pewters began to fly, and afterwards the long streets were vocal with various versions of what the girl had really told the soldier, and I went to bed murmuring: "I have found my destiny."

But it needs a more mighty intellect to write the Songs of the People. Some day a man will rise up from Bermondsey, Battersea or Bow, and he will be coarse, but clearsighted, hard but infinitely and tenderly humorous, speaking the people's tongue, steeped in their lives and telling them in swinging, urging, dinging verse what it is that their inarticulate lips would express. He will make them songs. Such songs! And all the little poets who pretend to sing to the people will scuttle away like rabbits, for the girl (which, as you have seen, of course, is wisdom) will tell that soldier (which is Hercules bowed under his labours) all that she knows of Life and Death and Love.

And the same, they say, is a Vulgarity!

The Betrayal of Confidences

That was its real name, and its nature was like unto it; but what else could I do? You must judge for me. They brought a card—the housemaid with the fan-teeth held it gingerly between black finger and blacker thumb—and it carried the name Mr. R. H. Hoffer in old Gothic letters. A hasty rush through the file of bills showed me that I owed nothing to any Mr. Hoffer, and assuming my sweetest smile, I bade Fan of the Teeth show him up. Enter stumblingly an entirely canary-coloured young person about twenty years of age, with a suspicious bulge in the bosom of his coat. He had grown no hair on his face; his eyes were of a delicate water-green, and his hat was a brown billycock, which he fingered nervously. As the room was blue with tobacco-smoke (and Latakia at that) he coughed even more nervously, and began seeking for me. I hid behind the writing-table and took notes. What I most noted was the bulge in his bosom. When a man begins to bulge as to that portion of his anatomy, hit him in the eye, for reason which will be apparent later on.

He saw me and advanced timidly. I invited him seductively to the only other chair, and "What's the trouble?" said I.

"I wanted to see you," said he.

"I am me." said I.

"I—I—I thought you would be quite otherwise," said he.

"I am, on the contrary, completely this way," said I. "Sit still, take your time and tell me all about it."

He wriggled tremulously for three minutes, and coughed again. I surveyed him, and waited developments. The bulge under his bosom crackled. Then I frowned. At the end of three minutes he began.

"I wanted to see what you were like," said he.

I inclined my head stiffly, as though all London habitually climbed the storeys on the same errand and rather worried me.

Then he delivered himself of a speech which he had evidently got by heart. He flushed painfully in the delivery.

"I am flattered," I said at the conclusion. "It is beastly gratifying. What do you want?"

"Advice if you will be so good." said the young man.

"Then you had better go somewhere else," said I.

The young man turned pink. "But I thought, after I had read your works—all your works, on my word—I had hoped that you would understand me, and I really have come for advice." The bulge crackled more ominously than ever.

"I understand perfectly," said I. "You are oppressed with vague and nameless longings, are you not?"

"I am terribly," said he.

"You do not wish to be as other men are? You desire to emerge from the common herd, to make your mark, and so forth?"

"Yes," said he in an awestricken whisper. "That is my desire."

"Also," said I, "you love, excessively, in several places at once cooks, housemaids, governesses, schoolgirls, and the aunts of other people."

"But one only," said he, and the pink deepened to beetroot.

"Consequently," said I, "you have written much—you have written verses."

"It was to teach me to write prose, only to teach me to write prose," he murmured. "You do it yourself, because I have bought your works—all your works."

He spoke as if he had purchased dunghills en bloc.

"We will waive that question," I said loftily. "Produce the verses."

"They—they aren't exactly verses," said the young man, plunging his hand into his bosom.

"I beg your pardon, I meant will you be good enough to read your five-act tragedy."

"How—how in the world did you know?" said the young man, more impressed than ever.

He unearthed his tragedy, the title of which I have given, and began to read. I felt as though I were walking in a dream; having been till then ignorant of the fact that earth held young men who held five-act tragedies in their insides. The young man gave me the whole of the performance, from the preliminary scene, where nothing more than an eruption of Vesuvius occurs to mar the serenity of the manager, till the very end, where the Roman sentry of Pompeii is slowly banked up with ashes in the presence of the audience, and dies murmuring through his helmet-vizor: "S.P. Q.R.R.I.P.R.S.V.P.," or words to that effect.

For three hours and one-half he read to me. And then I made a mistake.

"Sir," said I, "who's your Ma and Pa?"

"I haven't got any," said he, and his lower lip quivered.

"Where do you live?" I said.

"At the back of Tarporley Mews," said he.

"How?" said I.

"On eleven shillings a week," said he.

"I was pretty well educated, and if you don't stay too long they will let you read the books in the Holywell Street stalls."

"And you wasted your money buying my books," said I with a lump the size of a bolster in my throat.

"I got them second-hand, four and sixpence," said he, "and some I borrowed."

Then I collapsed. I didn't weep, but I took the tragedy and put it in the fire, and called myself every name that I knew.

This caused the young man to sob audibly, partly from emotion and partly from lack of food.

I took off my hat to him before I showed him out, and we went to a restaurant and I arranged things generally on a financial basis.

Would that I could let the tale stop here. But I cannot.

Three days later a man came to see me on business, an objectionable man of uncompromising truth. Just before he departed he said: "D' you know anything about the struggling author of a tragedy called 'The Betrayal of Confidences'?"

"Yes," said I. "One of the few poor souls who in the teeth of grinding poverty keep alight."

"At the back of Tarporley Mews," said he. "On eleven shillings a week."

"On the mischief!" said I.

"He didn't happen to tell you that he considered you the finest, subtlest, truest, and so forth of all the living so forths, did he?"

"He may have said something out of the fulness of an overladen heart. You know how unbridled is the enthusiasm of—"

"Young gentlemen who buy your books with their last farthing. You didn't soak it all in by any chance, give him a good meal and half a sovereign as well, did you?"

"I own up," I said. "I did all that and more. But how do you know?"

"Because he victimised me in the same way a fortnight ago."

"Thank you for that," I said, "but I burned his disgusting manuscripts. And he wept."

"There, unless he keeps a duplicate, you have scored one."

But considering the matter impartially, it seems to me that the game is not more than "fifteen all" in any light.

It makes me blush to think about it.

London in a Fog—November

Things have happened—but that is neither here nor there. What I urgently require is a servant—a nice, fat Mussulman khitmatgar, who is not above doing bearer's work on occasion. Such a man I would go down to Southampton or Tilbury to meet, would usher tenderly into a first-class carriage (I always go third myself) , and wrap in the warmest of flannel. He should be "Jenab;' and I would be "O Tum." When he died, as he assuredly would in this weather, I would bury him in my best back garden and write mortuary verses for publication in the Koh-i-Nur, or whatever vernacular paper he might read. I want, in short, a servant; and this is why I am writing to you.

The English, who, by the way, are unmitigated barbarians, maintain cotton-print housemaids to do work which is the manifest portion of a man. Besides which, no properly constructed person cares to see a white woman waiting upon his needs, filling coal-scuttles (these are very mysterious beasts) and tidying rooms. The young homebred Englishman does not object, and one of the most tantalising sights in the world is that of the young man of the house—the son newly introduced to shaving-water and great on the subject of maintaining authority—it is tantalising, I say, to see this young cub hectoring a miserable little slavey for not having lighted a fire or put his slippers in their proper place. The next time a big, bold man from the frontier comes home I shall hire him to kick a few young gentlemen of my acquaintance all round their own drawing-rooms while I lecture on my theory that this sort of thing accounts for the perceptible lack of chivalry in the modem Englishman. Now, if you or I or anybody else raved over and lectured at Kadir Baksh, or Ram Singh, or Jagesa on the necessity of obeying orders and the beauty of reverencing our noble selves, our men would laugh; or if the lecture struck them as too long-winded would ask us if our livers were out of order and recommend dawai. The housemaid must stand with her eyes on the ground while the young whelp sticks his hands under the tail of his dressing-gown and explains her duty to her. This makes me ill and sick—sick for Kadir Baksh, who rose from the earth when I called him, who knew the sequence of my papers and the ordering of my paltry garments, and, I verily believed, loved me not altogether for the sake of lucre. He said he would come with me to Belait because, "though the sahib says he will never return to India, yet I know, and all the other nauker log know, that return is his fate."

Being a fool, I left Kadir Baksh behind, and now I am alone with housemaids, who will under no circumstances sleep on the mat outside the door. Even as I write, one of these persons is cleaning up my room. Kadir Baksh would have done his work without noise. She tramps and scuffles; and, what is much worse, snuffles horribly. Kadir Baksh would have saluted me cheerfully and began some sort of a yam of the "It hath reached me, O Auspicious King!" order, and perhaps we should have debated over the worthlessness of Dunni, the sais, or the chances of a little cold-weather expedition, or the wisdom of retaining a fresh chaprassi—some intimate friend of Kadir Baksh. But now I have no horses and no chaprassis, and this smutty-faced girl glares at me across the room as though she expected I was going to eat her.

She must have a soul of her own—a life of her own—and perhaps a few amusements. I can't get at these things. She says: "Ho, yuss," and "Ho, no," and if I hadn't heard her chattering to the lift-boy on the stairs I should think that her education stopped at these two phrases. Now, I knew all about Kadir Baksh, his hopes and his savings—his experiences in the past, and the health of the little ones. He was a man—a human man remarkably like myself, and he knew that as well as I. A housemaid is of course not a man, but she might at least be a woman. My wanderings about this amazing heathen city have brought me into contact with very many English mem sahibs who seem to be eaten up with the fear of letting their servants get "above their position," or "presume," or do something which would shake the foundations of the four-mile cab radius. They seem to carry on a sort of cat-and-mouse war when the husband is at office and they have nothing much to do. Later, at places where their friends assemble, they recount the campaign, and the other women purr approvingly and say: "You did quite right, my dear. It is evident that she forgets her place."

All this is edifying to the stranger, and gives him a great idea of the dignity that has to be bolstered and buttressed, eight hours of the twenty-four, against the incendiary attacks of an eighteen-pound including-beer-money sleeps-in-a-garret-at-the-top-of-the-house servant-girl. There is a fine-crusted, slave-holding instinct in the hearts of a good many deep-bosomed matrons—a "throw back" to the times when we trafficked in black ivory. At tea-tables and places where they eat muffins it is called dignity. Now, your Kadir Baksh or my Kadir Baksh, who is a downtrodden and oppressed heathen (the young gentlemen who bullyrag white women assure me that we are in the habit of kicking our dependents and beating them with umbrellas daily), would ask for his chits, and probably say something sarcastic ere he drifted out of the compound gate, if you nagged or worried his noble self. He does not know much about the meaner forms of dignity, but he is entirely sound on the subject of izzat; and the fact of his cracking an azure and Oriental jest with you in the privacy of your dressing-room, or seeing you at your incoherent worst when you have an attack of fever, does not in the least affect his general deportment in public, where he knows that the honour of his sahib is his own honour, and dons a new kummerbund on the strength of it.

I have tried to deal with those housemaids in every possible way. To sling a blunt "Annie" or "Mary" or "Jane" at a girl whose only fault is that she is a heavy-handed incompetent, strikes me as rather an insult, seeing that the girl may have a brother, and that if you had a sister who was a servant you would object to her being howled at upstairs and downstairs by her given name. But only ladies' maids are entitled to their surnames. They are not nice people as a castee, and they regard the housemaids as the chamar regards the mehter. Consequently, I have to call these girls by their Christian names, and cock my feet up on a chair when they are cleaning the grate, and pass them in the halls in the morning as though they didn't exist. Now, the morning salutation of your Kadir Baksh or my Kadir is a performance which Turveydrop might envy. These persons don't understand a nod; they think it as bad as a wink, I believe. Respect and courtesy are lost upon them, and I suppose I must gather my dressing-gown into a tail and swear at them in the bloodless voice affected by the British female who—have I mentioned this?—is a highly composite heathen when she comes in contact with her sister clay downstairs.

The softer methods lay one open to harder suspicions. Not long ago there was trouble among my shirts. I fancied buttons grew on neck-bands. Kadir Baksh and the durzie encoraged me in the belief. When the lead-coloured linen (they cannot wash, by the way, in this stronghold of infidels) shed its buttons I cast about for a means of renewal. There was a housemaid, and she was not very ugly, and I thought she could sew. I knew I could not. Therefore I strove to ingratiate myself with her, believing that a little interest, combined with a little capital, would fix those buttons more firmly than anything else. Subsequently, and after an interval—the buttons were dropping like autumn leaves—I kissed her. The buttons were attached at once. So, unluckily, was the housemaid, for I gathered that she looked forward to a lifetime of shirtsewing in an official capacity, and my Revenue Board contemplated no additional establishment. My shirts are buttonsome, but my character is blasted. Oh, I wish I had Kadir Baksh!

This is only the first instalment of my troubles. The heathen in these parts do not understand me; so if you will allow I will come to you for sympathy from time to time. I am a child of calamity.

The New Dispensation—II

Writing of Kadir Baksh so wrought up my feelings that I could not rest till I had at least made an attempt to get a budli of some sort. The black man is essential to my comfort. I fancied I might in this city of barbarism catch a broken-down native strayed from his home and friends, who would be my friend and humble pardner—the sort of man, y' know, who would sleep on a rug somewhere near my chambers (I have forty things to tell you about chambers, but they come later), and generally look after my things. In the intervals of labour I would talk to him in his own tongue, and we would go abroad together and explore London. Do you know the Albert Docks? The British-India steamers go thence to the sunshine.

They sometimes leave a lascar or two on the wharf, and, in fact, the general tone of the population thereabouts is brown and umber. I was in no case to be particular. Anything dusky would do for me, so long as it could talk Hindustani and sew buttons. I went to the docks and walked about generally among the railway lines and packing-cases, till I found a man selling tooth-combs, which is not a paying trade. He was ragged even to furriness, and very unwashed. But he came from the East. "What are you?" I said, and the look of the missionary that steals over me in moments of agitation deluded that tooth-comb man into answering, "Sar, I am native ki-listi-an," but he put five more syllables into the last word.

There is no Christianity in the docks worth a tooth-comb. "I don't want your beliefs. I want your jat," said I.

"I am Tamil," said he, "and my name is Ramasawmy."

It was an awful thing to lower oneself to the level of a Colonel of the Madras Army, and come down to being tended by a Ramasawmy; but beggars cannot be choosers. I pointed out to him that the tooth-comb trade was a thing lightly to be dropped and taken up. He might injure his health by a washing, but he could not much hurt his prospects by coming along with me and trying his hand at bearer's work. "Could he work?" Oh, yes, he didn't mind work. He had been a servant in his time. Several servants, in fact.

"Could he wash himself?"

"Ye-es," he might do that if I gave him a coat—a thick coat—afterwards, and especially took care of the tooth-combs, for they were his little all.

"Had he any character of any kind?"'

He thought for a minute and then said cheerfully: "Not a little dam." Thereat I loved him, because a man who can speak the truth in minor matters may be trusted with important things, such as shirts.

We went home together till we struck a public bath, mercifully divided into three classes. I got him to go into the third without much difficulty. When he came out he was in the way of cleanliness, and before he had time to expostulate I ran him into the second. Into the first he would not go till I had bought him a cheap ulster. He came out almost clean. That cost me three shillings altogether. The ulster was half a sovereign, and some other clothes were thirty shillings. Even these things could not hide from me that he looked an unusually villainous creature.

At the chambers the trouble began. The people in charge had race prejudices very strongly, and I had to point out that he was a civilised native Christian anxious to improve his English—it was fluent but unchastened—before they would give him some sort of a crib to lie down in. The housemaids called him the Camel. I introduced him as "the Tamil," but they knew nothing of the ethnological subdivisions of India. They called him "that there beastly camel," and I saw by the light in his eye he understood only too well.

Coming up the staircase he confided to me his views about the housemaids. He had lived at the docks too long. I said they weren't. He said they were.

Then I showed him his duties, and he stood long in thought before the wardrobe. He evidently knew more than a little of the work, but whenever he came to a more than unusually dilapidated garment, he said: "No good for you, I take"; and he took. Then he put all the buttons on in the smoking of a pipe, and asked if there was anything else. I weakly said "No." He said: "Good-bye," and faded out of the house. The housekeeper of the chambers said he would never return.

But he did. At three in the morning home he came, and, naturally, possessing no latchkey, rang the bell. A policeman interfered, taking him for a burglar, and I was roused by the racket. I explained he was my servant, and the policeman said: "He do swear wonderful. 'Tain't any language. I know most of it, but some I've heard at Poplar." Then I dragged the Camel upstairs. He was quite sober, and said he had been waiting at the docks. He must wait at the docks every time a British-India steamer came in. A lascar on the Rewah had stabbed him in the side three voyages ago, and he was waiting for his man. "Maybe he have died," he said; "but if he have not died I catch him and cut his liver out." Then he curled himself up on the mat, and slept as noiselessly as a child.

Next morning he inspected the humble breakfast bloater, which did not meet with his approval, for he instantly cut it in two pieces, fried it with butter, dusted it with pepper, and miraculously made of it a dish fit for a king. When the shock-headed boy came to take away the breakfast things, he counted every piece of crockery into his quaking hand and said: "If you break one dam thing I cut your dam liver out and fly him with butter." Consequently, the housemaids said they were not going to clean the rooms as long as the Camel abode within. The Camel put his head out of the door and said they need not. He cleaned the rooms with his own hand and without noise, filled my pipe, made the bed, filled a pipe for himself, and sat down on the hearth-rug while I worked. When thought carried him away to the lascar of the Rewah, he would brandish the poker or take out his knife and whet it on the brickwork of the grate. It was a soothing sound to work to. At one o'clock he said that the Chyebassa would be in, and he must go. He demanded no money, saw that my tiffin was served, and fled. He returned at six o'clock singing a hymn. A lascar on the Chyebassa had told him that the Rewah was due in four days, and that his friend was not dead, but ripe for the knife. That night he got very drunk while I was out, and frightened the housemaids. All the chambers were in an uproar, but he crawled out of the skylight on the roof, and sat there till I came home.

In the dawn he was very penitent. He had misarranged his drink: the original intention being to sleep it off on my hearth-rug, but a housemaid had invited a friend up to the chambers to look at him, and the whispered comments and giggles made him angry. All next day he was restless but attentive. He urged me to fly to foreign shores, and take him with me. When other inducements failed, he reiterated that he was a "native ki-lis-ti-an," and whetted his knife more furiously than ever. "You do not like this place, I do not like this place. Let us travel dam quick. Let us go on the sea. I cook blotters." I told him this was impossible, but that if he stayed in my service we might later go abroad and enjoy ourselves.

But he would not rest and sleep on the rug and tend my shirts. On the morning of the Rewah's arrival he went away, and from his absence I fancied he had fallen into the hands of the law. But at midnight he came back, weak and husky.

"Have got him," said he simply, and dragged his ulster down from the wall, wrapping it very tightly round him. "Now I go 'way."

He went into the bedroom, and began counting over the tale of the week's wash, the boots, and so forth. "All right," he called into the other room. Then came in to say good-bye, walking slowly.

"What's your name, marshter?" said he. I told him. He bowed and descended the staircase painfully. I had not paid him a penny, and since he did not ask for it, counted on his returning at least for wages.

It was not till next morning that I found big dark drops on most of my clean shirts, and the housemaid complained of a trail of blood all down the staircase.

"The Camel" had received payment in full from other hands than mine.

The Last of the Stories

Wherefore I perceive that there is nothing better than that a man should rejoice in his own works; for that is his portion.
—Ecc. iii, 22.

"Kench with a long hand, lazy one," I said to the punkah coolie. "But I am tired," said the coolie. "Then go to Jehannum and get another man to pull," I replied, which was rude and, when you come to think of it, unnecessary.

"Happy thought—go to Jehannum!" said a voice at my elbow. I turned and saw, seated on the edge of my bed, a large and luminous Devil. "I'm not afraid," I said. "You're an illusion bred by too much tobacco and not enough sleep. If I look at you steadily for a minute you will disappear. You are an ignis fatuus."

"Fatuous yourself!" answered the Devil blandly. "Do you mean to say you don't know me?" He shrivelled up to the size of a blob of sediment on the end of a pen, and I recognised my old friend the Devil of Discontent, who lived in the bottom of the inkpot, but emerges half a day after each story has been printed with a host of useless suggestions for its betterment.

"Oh, it's you, is it?" I said. "You're not due till next week. Get back to your inkpot."

"Hush!" said the Devil. "I have an idea."

"Too late, as usual. I know your ways."

"No. It's a perfectly practicable one. Your swearing at the coolie suggested it. Did you ever hear of a man called Dante—ch'armin' fellow, friend o' mine?"

" 'Dante once prepared to paint a picture,' I quoted.

"Yes. I inspired that notion—but never mind. Are you willing to play Dante to my Virgil? I can't guarantee a nine-circle Inferno, any more than you can turn out a cantoed epic, but there's absolutely no risk and—it will run to three columns at least."

"But what sort of Hell do you own?" I said. I fancied your operations were mostly above ground. You have no jurisdiction over the dead.

"Sainted Leopardi!" rapped the Devil, resuming natural size. "Is that all you know? I'm proprietor of one of the largest Hells in existence—the Limbo of Lost Endeavor, where the souls of all the Characters go."

"Characters? What Characters?"

"All the characters that are drawn in books, painted in novels, sketched in magazine articles, thumbnailed in feuilletons or in any way created by anybody and everybody who has had the fortune or misfortune to put his or her writings into print."

"That sounds like a quotation from a prospectus. What do you herd Characters for? Aren't there enough souls in the Universe?"

"Who possess souls and who do not? For aught you can prove, man may be soulless and the creatures he writes about immortal. Anyhow, about a hundred years after printing became an established nuisance, the loose Characters used to blow about interplanetary space in legions which interfered with traffic. So they were collected, and their charge became mine by right. Would you care to see them? Your own are there."

"That decides me. But is it hotter than Northern India?"

"On my Devildom, no. Put your arms round my neck and sit tight. I'm going to dive!"

He plunged from the bed headfirst into the floor. There was a smell of jail-durrie and damp earth; and then fell the black darkness of night.

We stood before a door in a topless wall, from the further side of which came faintly the roar of infernal fires.

"But you said there was no danger!" I cried in an extremity of terror.

"No more there is," said the Devil. "That's only the Furnace of First Edition. Will you go on? No other human being has set foot here in the flesh. Let me bring the door to your notice. Pretty design, isn't it? A joke of the Master's."

I shuddered, for the door was nothing more than 8 coffin, the backboard knocked out, set on end in the thickness of the wall. As I hesitated, the silence of space was cut by a sharp, shrill whistle, like that of a live shell, which rapidly grew louder and louder. "Get away from the door," said the Devil of Discontent quickly. "Here's a soul coming to its place." I took refuge under the broad vans of the Devil's wings. The whistle rose to an ear-splitting shriek and a naked soul flashed past me.

"Always the same," said the Devil quietly. "These little writers are so anxious to reach their reward. H'm, I don't think he likes his'n, though." A yell of despair reached my ears and I shuddered afresh. "Who was he?" I asked. "Hack-writer for a pornographic firm in Belgium, exporting to London, you'll understand presently—and now we'll go in," said the Devil. "I must apologise for that creature's rudeness. He should have stopped at the distance-signal for line-clear. You can hear the souls whistling there now."

"Are they the souls of men?" I whispered.

"Yes—writer-men. That's why they are so shrill and querulous. Welcome to the Limbo of Lost Endeavour!"

They passed into a domed hall, more vast than visions could embrace, crowded to its limit by men, women and children. Round the eye of the dome ran, a flickering fire, that terrible quotation from Job: "Oh, that mine enemy had written a book!"

"Neat, isn't it?" said the Devil, following my glance. "Another joke of the Master's. Man of Us, y' know. In the old days we used to put the Characters into a disused circle of Dante's Inferno, but they grew overcrowded. So Balzac and Théophile Gautier were commissioned to write up this building. It took them three years to complete, and is one of the finest under earth. Don't attempt to describe it unless you are quite sure you are equal to Balzac and Gautier in collaboration. "Look at the crowds and tell me what you think of them."

I looked long and earnestly, and saw that many of the multitude were cripples. They walked on their heels or their toes, or with a list to the right or left. A few of them possessed odd eyes and parti-coloured hair; more threw themselves into absurd and impossible attitudes; and every fourth woman seemed to be weeping.

"Who are these?" I said.

"Mainly the population of three-volume novels that never reach the six-shilling stage. See that beautiful girl with one grey eye and one brown, and the black and yellow hair? Let her be an awful warning to you how you correct your proofs. She was created by a careless writer a month ago, and he changed all colours in the second volume. So she came here as you see her. There will be trouble when she meets her author. He can't alter her now, and she says she'll accept no apology."

"But when will she meet her author?"

"Not in my department. Do you notice a general air of expectancy among all the Characters? They are waiting for their authors. Look! That explains the system better than I can."

A lovely maiden, at whose feet I would willingly have fallen and worshipped, detached herself from the crowd and hastened to the door through which I had just come. There was a prolonged whistle without, a soul dashed through the coffin and fell upon her neck. The girl with the parti-coloured hair eyed the couple enviously as they departed arm in arm to the other side of the hall.

"That man," said the Devil, "wrote one magazine story, of twenty-four pages, ten years ago when he was desperately in love with a flesh and blood woman. He put all his heart into the work, and created the girl you have just seen. The flesh and blood woman married some one else and died—it's a way they have—but the man has this girl for his very own, and she will everlastingly grow sweeter."

"Then the Characters are independent?"

"Slightly! Have you never known one of your Characters—even yours—get beyond control as soon as they are made?"

"That's true. Where are those two happy creatures going?"

"To the Levels. You've heard of authors finding their levels? We keep all the Levels here. As each writer enters, he picks up his Characters, or they pick him up, as the case may be, and to the Levels he goes."

"I should like to see—"

"So you shall, when you come through that door a second time—whistling. I can't take you there now."

"Do you keep only the Characters of living scribblers in this hall?"

"We should be crowded out if we didn't draft them off somehow. Step this way and I'll take you to the Master. One moment, though. There's John Ridd with Lorna Doone, and there are Mr. Maliphant and the Bormalacks—clannish folk, those Besant Characters—don't let the twins talk to you about Literature and Art. Come along. What's here?"

The white face of Mr. John Oakhurst, gambler, broke through the press. "I wish to explain," said he in a level voice, "that had I been consulted I should never have blown out my brains with the Duchess and all that Poker Flat lot. I wish to add that the only woman I ever loved was the wife of Brown of Calaveras." He pressed his hand behind him suggestively. "All right, Mr. Oakhurst," I said hastily; "I believe you." "Kin you set it right?" he asked, dropping into the Doric of the Gulches. I caught a trigger's cloth-muffled click. "Just heavens!" I groaned. "Must I be shot for the sake of another man's Characters?" Oakhurst levelled his revolver at my head, but the weapon was struck up by the hand of Yuba Bill. "You damned fool!" said the stage-driver. "Haven't I told you no one but a blamed idiot shoots at sight now? Let the galoot go. You kin see by his eyes he's no party to your matrimonial arrangements." Oakhurst retired with an irreproachable bow, but in my haste to escape I fell over Caliban, his head in a melon and his tame orc under his arm. He spat like a wildcat.

"Manners none, customs beastly," said the Devil. "We'll take the Bishop with us. They all respect the Bishop." And the great Bishop Blougram joined us, calm and smiling, with the news, for my private ear, that Mr. Gigadibs despised him no longer.

We were arrested by a knot of semi-nude Bacchantes kissing a clergyman. The Bishop's eyes twinkled, and I turned to the Devil for explanation.

"That's Robert Elsmere—what's left of him," said the Devil. "Those are French feuilleton women and scourings of the Opera Comique. He has been lecturing 'em, and they don't like it." "He lectured me!" said the Bishop with a bland smile. "He has been a nuisance ever since he came here. By the Holy Law of Proportion, he had the audacity to talk to the Master! Called him a 'pot-bellied barbarian'! That is why he is walking so stiffly now," said the Devil. "Listen! Marie Pigeonnier is swearing deathless love to him. On my word, we ought to segregate the French characters entirely. By the way, your regiment came in very handy for Zola's importations."

"My regiment?" I said. "How do you mean?"

"You wrote something about the Tyneside Tail-Twisters, just enough to give the outline of the regiment, and of course it came down here—one thousand and eighty strong. I told it off in hollow squares to pen up the Rougon-Macquart series. There they are." I looked and saw the Tyneside Tail-Twisters ringing an inferno of struggling, shouting, blaspheming men and women in the costumes of the Second Empire.

Now and again the shadowy ranks brought down their butts on the toes of the crowd inside the square, and shrieks of pain followed. "You should have indicated your men more clearly; they are hardly up to their work," said the Devil. "If the Zola tribe increase, I'm afraid I shall have to use up your two companies of the Black Tyrone and two of the Old Regiment."

"I am proud—" I began.

"Go slow," said the Devil. "You won't be half so proud in a little while, and I don't think much of your regiments, anyway. But they are good enough to fight the French. Can you hear Coupeau raving in the left angle of the square? He used to run about the hall seeing pink snakes, till the children's story-book Characters protested. Come along!"

Never since Caxton pulled his first proof and made for the world a new and most terrible God of Labour had mortal man such an experience as mine when I followed the Devil of Discontent through the shifting crowds below the motto of the Dome. A few—a very few—of the faces were of old friends, but there were thousands whom I did not recognise. Men in every conceivable attire and of every possible nationality, deformed by intention, or the impotence of creation that could not create—blind, unclean, heroic, mad, sinking under the weight of remorse, or with eyes made splendid by the light of love and fixed endeavour; women fashioned in ignorance and mourning the errors of their creator, life and thought at variance with body and soul; perfect women such as walk rarely upon this earth, and horrors that were women only because they had not sufficient self-control to be fiends; little children, fair as the morning, who put their hands into mine and made most innocent confidences; loathsome, lank-haired infant-saints, curious as to the welfare of my soul, and delightfully mischievous boys, generalled by the irrepressible Tom Sawyer, who played among murderers, harlots, professional beauties, nuns, Italian bandits and politicians of state.

The ordered peace of Arthur's Court was broken up by the incursions of Mr. John Wellington Wells, and Dagonet, the jester, found that his antics drew no attention so long as the "dealer in magic and spells," taking Tristram's harp, sang patter-songs to the Round Table; while a Zulu Impi, headed by Allan Quatermain, wheeled and shouted in sham fight for the pleasure of Little Lord Fauntleroy. Every century and every type was jumbled in the confusion of one colossal fancy hall where all the characters were living their parts.

"Aye, look long," said the Devil. "You will never be able to describe it, and the next time you come you won't have the chance. Look long, and look at"—Good's passing with a maiden of the Zu-Vendi must have suggested the idea—"look at their legs," I looked, and for the second time noticed the lameness that seemed to be almost universal in the Limbo of Lost Endeavour. Brave men and stalwart to all appearance had one leg shorter than the other; some paced a few inches above the floor, never touching it, and others found the greatest difficulty in preserving their feet at all. The stiffness and laboured gait of these thousands was pitiful to witness. I was sorry for them. I told the Devil as much.

"H'm," said he reflectively, "that's the world's work. Rather cockeye, ain't it? They do everything but stand on their feet. You could improve them, I suppose?" There was an unpleasant sneer in his tone, and I hastened to change the subject.

"I'm tired of walking," I said. "I want to see some of my own Characters, and go on to the Master, whoever he may be, afterwards."

"Reflect," said the Devil. "Are you certain—do you know how many they be?"

"No—but I want to see them. That's what I came for."

"Very well. Don't abuse me if you don't like the view. There are one-and-fifty of your make up to date, and—it's rather an appalling thing to be confronted with fifty-one children. However, here's a special favourite of yours. Go and shake hands with her!"

A limp-jointed, staring-eyed doll was hirpling towards me with a strained smile of recognition. I felt that I knew her only too well—if indeed she were she. "Keep her off. Devil!" I cried, stepping back. "I never made that!" "'She began to weep and she began to cry. Lord ha' mercy on me, this is none of I!' You're very rude to—Mrs. Hauksbee, and she wants to speak to you," said the Devil. My face must have betrayed my dismay, for the Devil went on soothingly: "That's as she is, remember. I knew you wouldn't like it. Now what will you give if I make her as she ought to be? No, I don't want your soul, thanks. I have it already, and many others of better quality. Will you, when you write your story, own that I am the best and greatest of all the Devils?" The doll was creeping nearer. "Yes," I said hurriedly. "Anything you like. Only I can't stand her in that state."

"You'll have to when you come next again. Look! No connection with Jekyll and Hyde!" The Devil pointed a lean and inky finger towards the doll, and lo! radiant, bewitching, with a smile of dainty malice, her high heels clicking on the floor like castanets, advanced Mrs. Hauksbee as I had imagined her in the beginning.

"Ah!" she said. "You are here so soon? Not dead yet? That will come. Meantime, a thousand congratulations. And now, what do you think of me?" She put her hands on her hips, revealed a glimpse of the smallest foot in Simla and hummed: "'Just look at that—just look at this! And then you'll see I'm not amiss.'"

"She'll use exactly the same words when you meet her next time," said the Devil warningly, "You dowered her with any amount of vanity, if you left out—Excuse me a minute! I'll fetch up the rest of your menagerie." Cut I was looking at Mrs. Hauksbee.

"Well?" she said. "Am I what you expected?" I forgot the Devil and all his works, forgot that this was not the woman I had made, could only murmur rapturously: "by Jove! You are a beauty." Then incautiously: "And you stand on your feet." "Good heavens!" said Mrs. Hauksbee. "Would you, at my time of life, have me stand on my head?" She folded her arms and looked me up and down. I was grinning imbecilely" the woman was so alive. "Talk," I said absently; "I want to hear you talk." "I am not used to being spoken to like a coolie," she replied. "Never mid," I said, "that may be right for outsiders, but I made you and I've a right—"

"You have a right? You made me? My dear sir, if I didn't know that we would bore each other so inextinguishable hereafter I should read you an hour's lecture this instant. You made me! I suppose you will have the audacity to pretend that you understand me—that you ever understood me. Oh, man, man—foolish man! If only you knew!"

"Is that the person who thinks he understood us, Loo?" drawled a voice at her elbow. The devil had returned with a cloud of witnesses, and it was Mrs. Mallowe who was speaking.

"I've touched 'em all up," said the Devil in an aside. "You couldn't stand 'em raw. But don't run away with the notion that they are your work. I show you what they ought to be. You must find out for yourself how to make 'em so."

"Am I allowed to remodel the batch—up above?" I asked anxiously.

"Litera scripta manet. That's in the Delectus and Eternity." He turned round to the semi-circle of Characters: "Ladies and gentlemen, who are all a great deal better than you should be by virtue of my power, let me introduce you to your maker. If you have anything to say to him, you can say it."

"What insolence!" said Mrs. Hauksbee between her teeth. "This isn't a Peterhoff drawing-room. I haven't the slightest intention of being leveed by this person. Polly, come here and we'll watch the animals go by." She and Mrs. Mallowe stood at my side. I turned crimson with shame, for it is an awful thing to see one's Characters in the solid.

"Wal," said Gilead P. Beck as he passed, "I would not be you at this pre-cise moment of time, not for all the ile in the univarsal airth. No, sirri I thought my dinner-party was soul-shatterin', but it's mush—mush and milk—to your circus. Let the good work go on!"

I turned to the company and saw that they were men and women, standing upon their feet as folks should stand. Again I forgot the Devil, who stood apart and sneered. From the distant door of entry I could hear the whistle of arriving souls, from the semi-darkness at the end of the hall came the thunderous roar of the Furnace of First Edition, and everywhere the restless crowds of Characters muttered and rustled like windblown autumn leaves. But I looked upon my own people and was perfectly content as man could be.

"I have seen you study a new dress with just such an expression of idiotic beatitude," whispered Mrs. Mallowe to Mrs. Hauksbee. "Hushl" said the latter. "He thinks he understands." Then to me: "Please trot them out. Eternity is long enough in all conscience, but that is no reason for wasting it. Pro-ceed, or shall I call them up? Mrs. Vansuythen, Mr. Boult, Mrs. Boult, Captain Kurrel and the Majorl" The European population in Kashima in the Dosehri hills, the actors in the Wayside Comedy, moved towards me; and I saw with delight that they were human. "So you wrote about us?" said Mrs. Boult. "About my confession to my husband aad my hatred of that Vansuythen woman? Did you think that you understood? Are all men such fools?" "That woman is bad form," said Mrs. Hauksbee, "but she speaks the truth. I wonder what these soldiers have to say," Gunner Barnabas and Private Shacklock stopped, saluted, and hoped I would take no offence if they gave it as their opinion that I had not "got them down quite right." I gasped.

A spurred Hussar succeeded, his wife on his arm. It was Captain Gadsby and Minnie, and close behind them swaggered Jack Mafflin, the Brigadier-General in his arms. "Had the cheek to try to describe our life, had you?" said Gadsby carelessly. "Ha-hmm! S'pose he understood, Minnie?" Mrs. Gadsby raised her face to her husband and murmured: "I'm sure he didn't, Pip," while Poor Dear Mamma, still in her riding-habit, hissed: "I'm sure he didn't understand me" And these also went their way.

One after another they filed by—Trewinnard, the pet of his Department; Otis Yeere, lean and lanthomjawed; Crook O'Neil and Bobby Wick arm in arm; Janki Meah, the blind miner in the Jimahari coal fields; Afzul Khan, the policeman; the murderous Fathan horse-dealer, Durga Dass; the bunnia, Boh Da Thone; the dacoit, Dana Da, weaver of false magic; the Leander of the Barhwi ford; Peg Barney, drunk as a coot; Mrs, Delville, the dowd; Dinah Shadd, large, red-cheeked and resolute; Simmons, Slane and Losson; Georgie Porgie and his Burmese helpmate; a shadow in a high collar, who was all that I had ever indicated of the Hawley Boy—the nameless men and women who had trod the Hill of Illusion and lived in the Tents of Eedar, and last, His Majesty the King.

Each one in passing told me the same tale, and the burden thereof was: "You did not understand." My heart turned sick within me. "Where's Wee Willie Winkie?" I shouted. "Little children don't lie."

A clatter of pony's feet followed, and the child appeared, habited as on the day he rode into Afghan territory to warn Coppy's love against the "bad men." "I've been playing," he sobbed, "playing on ve Levels wiv Jackanapes and Lollo, an' he says I'm only just borrowed. I'm isn't borrowed. I'm Willie Wi-inkie! Vere's Coppy?"

"'Out of the mouths of babes and sucklings'," whispered the Devil, who had drawn nearer. "You know the rest of the proverb. Don't look as if you were going to be shot in the morning! Here are the last of your gang."

I turned despairingly to the Three Musketeers, dearest of all my children to me—to Privates Mulvaney, Ortheris and Learoyd. Surely the Three would not turn against me as the others had done! I shook hands with Mulvaney. "Terence, how goes? Are you going to make fun of me, too?" "'Tis not for me to make fun av you, sorr," said the Irishman, "knowin' as I du know, fwat good friends we've been for the matter av three years."

"Fower," said Ortheris, "'twas in the Helanthami barricks, H block, we was become acquaint, an' 'ere's thankin' you kindly for all the beer we've drunk twix' that and now."

"Four ut is, then," said Mulvaney. "He an' Dinah Shadd are your friends, but—" He stood uneasily.

"But what?" I said.

"Savin' your presence, sorr, an' it's more than onwillin' I am to be hurtin' you; you did not ondersthand. On my sowl an' honour, sorr, you did not ondersthand. Come along, you two."

But Ortheris stayed for a moment to whisper: "It's Gawd's own trewth, but there's this 'ere to think. 'Tain't the bloomin' belt that's wrong, as Peg Barney sez, when he's up for bein' dirty on p'rade. 'Tain't the bloomin' belt, sir; it's the bloomin' pipeclay." Ere I could seek an explanation he had joined his companions.

"For a private soldier, a singularly shrewd man," said Mrs. Hauksbee, and she repeated Ortheris's words. The last drop filled my cup, and I am ashamed to say that I bade her be quiet in a wholly unjustifiable tone. I was rewarded by what would have been a notable lecture on propriety, had I not said to the Devil: "Change that woman to a damned doll again! Change 'em all back as they were—as they are. I'm sick of them."

"Poor wretch!" said the Devil of Discontent very quietly. "They are changed."

The reproof died on Mrs. Hauksbee's lips, and she moved away marionette-fashion, Mrs. Mallowe trailing after her. I hastened after the remainder of the Characters, and they were changed indeed—even as the Devil had said, who kept at my side.

They limped and stuttered and staggered and mouthed and staggered round me, till I could endure no more.

"So I am the master of this idiotic puppet show, am I?" I said bitterly, watching Mulvaney trying to come to attention by spasms.

"In saecula saeculorum," said the Devil, bowing his head; "and you needn't kick, my dear fellow, because they will concern no one but yourself by the time you whistle up to the door. Stop reviling me and uncover. Here's the Master!"

Uncover! I would have dropped on my knees, had not the Devil prevented me, at sight of the portly form of Maitre François Rabelais, some time Curé of Meudon. He wore a smoke-stained apron of the colour's of Gargantua. I made a sign which was duly returned. "An Entered Apprentice in difficulties with his rough ashlar, Worshipful Sir," explained the Devil. I was too angry to speak.

Said the Master, rubbing his chin: "Are those things yours?" "Even so. Worshipful Sir," I muttered, praying inwardly that the Characters would at least keep quiet while the Master was near. He touched one or two thoughtfully, put his hand upon my shoulder and started: "By the Great Bells of Notre Dame, you are in the flesh—the warm flesh!—the flesh I quitted so long—ah, so long! And you fret and behave unseemly because of these shadows! Listen now! I, even I, would give my Three, Panurge, Gargantua and Pantagruel, for one little hour of the life that is in you. And I am the Master!"

But the words gave me no comfort. I could hear Mrs. Mallowe's joints cracking—or it might have been merely her stays.

"Worshipful Sir, he will not believe that," said the Devil. "Who live by shadows lust for shadows. Tell him something more to his need."

The Master grunted contemptuously: "And he is flesh and blood! Know this, then. The First Law is to make them stand upon their feet, and the Second is to make them stand upon their feet, and the Third is to make them stand upon their feet. But, for all that, Trajan is a fisher of frogs." He passed on, and I could hear him say to himself: "One hour—one minute—of life in the flesh, and I would sell the Great Perhaps thrice over!"

"Well," said the Devil, "you've made the Master angry, seen about all there is to be seen, except the Furnace of First Edition, and, as the Master is in charge of that, I should avoid it. Now you'd better go. You know what you ought to do?"

"I don't need all Hell—"

"Pardon me. Better men than you have called this Paradise."

"All Hell, I said, and the Master to tell me what I knew before. What I want to know is how?" "Go and find out," said the Devil. We turned to the door, and I was aware that my Characters had grouped themselves at the exit. "They are going to give you an ovation. Think o' that, now!" said the Devil. I shuddered and dropped my eyes, while one-and-fifty voices broke into a wailing song, whereof the words, so far as I recollect, ran:

But we brought forth and reared in hours
Of change, alarm, surprise.
What shelter to grow ripe is ours—
What leisure to grow wise?

I ran the gauntlet, narrowly missed collision with an impetuous soul (I hoped he liked his Characters when he met them), and flung free into the night, where I should have knocked my head against the stars. But the Devil caught me.

The brain-fever bird was fluting across the grey, dewy lawn, and the punkah had stopped again. "Go to Jehannum and get another man to pull," I said drowsily. "Exactly," said a voice from the inkpot.

Now the proof that this story is absolutely true lies in the fact that there will be no other to follow it.

Rudyard Kipling – A Short Biography

Born in Bombay on 30th December 1865, Joseph Rudyard Kipling wrote short stories, poems and novels, a body of work whose reputation is in constant flux as his presentations and interpretations of empire are viewed within the changing context of empirical absolution in the twentieth century. Having spent the first five years of his life in India he felt a natural affinity for the country, though his upbringing had a distinctly colonial taste flavour. He was born in the Bombay Presidency of British India to Lockwood Kipling, an English art teacher and illustrator who took a position as professor of architectural sculpture in the Jeejeebhoy School of Art and Alice MacDonald, spoken of by the a Viceroy of India that "dullness and Mrs Kipling cannot exist in the same room". Though their presence in India was principally artistic and educational, rather than political, the company they kept and the establishments in which they kept it indicate an existence very much benefitting from the British Empire. Lockwood would later go on to assume a position as curator of the Lahore Museum, while working on various illustrations for Rudyard's writing, and various decorations for the Victoria and Albert museum in London. Much of his work, then, was coloured by the empire, whether in service to or benefitting from, and it was into this distinctly British experience of India that Rudyard was born.

Lockwood and Alice had met and fallen in love at Rudyard Lake in Rudyard, Staffordshire, and their affections for the area were so great they chose to refer to the lake in naming their first-born. Alice came from a family of four sisters, all of whose marriages were significant and well-arranged; moreover, Rudyard's most famous relative was Stanley Baldwin, Conservative Prime Minister on three occasions in the 1920s and 1930s. Kipling's sense of belonging in Bombay is found in 'To the City of Bombay' in the dedication to Seven Seas, a collection of poems published in 1900, which reads:—

> Mother of Cities to me,
> For I was born in her gate,
> Between the palms and the sea,
> Where the world-end steamers wait.

His parents considered themselves Anglo-Indians, and he would later assume this classification although he did not live there long. His first five years, which he describes as days of "strong light and darkness", ended when he and his three-year-old sister Alice were removed to Southsea, Plymouth, to board with Captain Pryse Agar Holloway and his wife Mrs Sarah Holloway, a couple who cared for the children of couples born in British India. They were there for six years and Kipling would later recall their time there with horror, describing incidents of cruelty and neglect and wondering whether it was these which speeded up his literary maturity, for "it made me give attention to the lies I soon found it necessary to tell: and this, I presume, is the foundation of literary effort".

Alice's time, by contrast, was relatively comfortable, Mrs Holloway hoping that she would marry her son, though this ambition would not come to fruition. They did have relatives in England, a maternal aunt Georgiana and her husband who lived in Fulham, London, in a house at which they spent a month each Christmas and which Kipling later described as "a paradise which I verily believe saved me". Their mother returned in 1877 and removed them from their custody with the Holloways. A year later he gained admission to the United Services College at Westward Ho! in Devon, a recently established school with the intention of readying boys for military service in the British Army. His time here was fraught physically, though emotionally it proved fruitful for he began several firm friendships with other boys at the school. Moreover, he found in it inspiration for the setting of his series of schoolboy stories, Stalky and Co, begun in 1899. Meanwhile, his sister Alice had returned to Southsea and was boarding with Florence Garrard, with whom he fell in love and on whom he modeled Maisie in his first novel, The Light That Failed, published in 1891. At sixteen he was found lacking in the academic perspicacity necessary to undertake a scholarship to Oxford University, his parents meanwhile lacking the wherewithal to finance him therein. As such his father sought a job for him in Lahore, Punjab, where he was now a museum curator. The position he found for his son was as assistant editor of the Civil and Military Gazette, a small local newspaper. Kipling left for India on 20th September 1882, arriving in Bombay on 18th October. "There were yet three or four days" rail to Lahore, where my people lived. After these, my English years fell away, nor ever, I think, came back in full strength".

The Gazette appeared six days of the week, year-round save for a short break at both Christmas and Easter. Its editor Stephen Wheeler was diligent but Kipling's writing was insatiable, and he came to consider the paper his "mistress and most true love". In the summer of 1883 Kipling visited Shimla, the colonial hill-station and summer capital of British India which was then called Simla. Chosen by the British owing to its resemblance of English climate and scenery (as far as was possible in India), it became the seat of the Viceroy of India for the six months on the plains which were too hot for the British temperament, and subsequently became a "centre of power as well as pleasure". Lockwood was asked to serve in the Church there, and his family became yearly visitors while Kipling himself would take his annual leave here from 1885-88. The value of this time is evident from the regularity with which Simla appears in his writing for the Gazette, which in his journals he describes the time as

> "….pure joy—every golden hour counted. It began in heat and discomfort, by rail and road. It ended in the cool evening, with a wood fire in one's bedroom, and next morn—thirty more of them ahead!—the early cup of tea, the Mother who brought it in, and the long talks of us all together again."

In 1886, his Departmental Ditties appeared, his first collection of verse, and brought with it a change of editor; Kay Robinson, Wheeler's replacement, was in favour of Kipling's creativity and granted him more freedom in that respect, even asking him to write short stories to appear in the newspaper. The vivacity of his writing was captured in a description of him by an ex-colleague at the Gazette, saying he "never knew such a fellow for ink—he simply revelled in it, filling up his pen viciously, and then throwing the contents all over the office, so that it was almost dangerous to approach him". While in Lahore, he had thirty-nine stories published in the Gazette between November 1886 and June 1887. Most of these are compiled in Plain Tales from the Hills, his first collection of prose, which was published in January 1888 in Calcutta, shortly after his 22nd birthday. In November 1887, he transferred from the Gazette to its much larger sister newspaper, The Pioneer, based in Allahabad. The pace of his writing remained, and in 1888 he published six collections of stories, Soldiers Three, The Story of the Gadsbys, In Black and White, Under the Deodars, The Phantom Rickshaw and Wee Willie Winkie, composed of some 41 stories. In addition, his position as The Pioneer's special correspondent in the Western region of Rajputna, he wrote many sketches which were later compiled in Letters of Marque and published in From Sea to Sea and Other Sketches, Letters of Travel.

A dispute in 1889 saw him discharged from The Pioneer, though by now he had been considering his future and sold the rights to his six volumes of stories for £200 and a small royalty, while the Plain Tales fetched £50, along with six months' salary from The Pioneer in lieu of notice. Using the money to undertake a pilgrimage to London, the literary centre of the British Empire, he left India on 9th March 1889, travelling via Rangoon, San Francisco, Hong Kong and Japan, then through the United States writing articles for The Pioneer which were also included in From Sea to Sea and Other Sketches, Letters of Travel. Arriving in England at Liverpool on October 1889, London and his literary début there beckoned.

His first task was to find a place to live, and he eventually settled on quarters in Villiers Street, Strand. The next two years saw several stories accepted by various magazine editors, the publication of the novel The Light That Failed, a nervous breakdown, the collaboration with Wolcott Balestier on the novel (uncharacterstically misspelt) The Naulhaka, and in 1891, following his doctors' advice, he embarked on a further sea voyage, travelling to South Africa, Australia, New Zealand and also returning to India. His plans to spend Christmas with his family were cut short on the news of Balestier's sudden death from typhoid fever, prompting an immediate return to London. Before he left, he had proposed to Balestier's sister Caroline Starr Balestier, with whom he had been having a hushed romance for just over a year. Back in London, Life's Handicap was published in 1891, a collection of short stories whose subject was the British in India, and British India. On 18th January 1892 aged 26 he married Caroline in the midst of an epidemic of influenza. Caroline was given away by Henry James, the famous and celebrated American author.

Honeymooning in Japan, they travelled via Vermont, America, to visit the Balestier estate, and upon arrival in Yokahama they found that their bank, The New Oriental Banking Corporation, had failed, though this loss did not deter them and they returned to Vermont, Caroline now pregnant with their first child. Renting a cottage on a farm for $10 per month, they lived a spartan existence and were "extraordinarily and self-centredly content". The named the residence Bliss Cottage, and it was here that the child was born, named Josephine, "in three foot of snow on the night of 29th December 1892. Her Mother's birthday being the 31st and mine the 30th we congratulated her on her sense of the fitness of things." While here, Kipling had his first ideas for the Jungle Books. Shortly after Josephine was born the couple moved in pursuit of more space and comfort, buying ten acres overlooking the Connecticut River from Caroline's brother. The house they built there was inspired by the Mughul architecture he encountered in Lahore, and was named Naulakha (this time correctly spelt) in honour of Wolcott. His literary output in four years here included the Jungle Books, a collection of short stories entitled The Day's Work, the novel Captain Courageous and a plethora of poetry, of which most notably the volume

The Seven Seas and his Barrack-Room Ballads. Meanwhile, he enjoyed correspondence with the many children who wrote to him about the Jungle Books.

In between this writing, Kipling took regular visitors. Most notably Arthur Conan Doyle came, bringing golf clubs and staying for two days to give Kipling an extended golf lesson. Kipling enjoyed the game so much that he continued to play, even in winter with special red balls, though he found that the ice would lead to drives travelling two miles as they slid "down the long slope to the Connecticut River". Elsie, the couple's second daughter, was born in February 1896, and by this time it is thought that their marriage had lost its original spark of spontaneity and descended into routine, though they remained loyal to one another. By now, failed arbitration between the United States and England over a border dispute involving British Guiana incited Anglo-American tensions which, in May 1896, resulted in a confrontation between Kipling and Caroline's brother, resulting in his arrest and, in the hearing which followed, the destruction of Kipling's private life, leaving him exhausted and miserable and leading to their return to England.

They had settled Torquay, Devon, by September 1896, and he remained socially present and literarily productive. The success of his writing had brought him fame, and he had responded with a sense of duty to include in his writing elements of political persuasion, most notably in his two poems Recessional and The White Man's Burden, which caused controversy when they were published in 1897 and 1899 respectively. Many considered them anthemic to the empire, propaganda for the imperial mindset so prevalent in the Victoria era. Their first son, John, was born in August 1887. Another journey to South Africa began a tradition of wintering there, which continued until 1908. His reputation as Poet of the Empire saw him well-received by politicians in the Cape Colony, and he started the newspaper The Friend for Lord Roberts and the British troops in Bloemfontein. Back in England, they moved to Rottingdean, East Sussex, in 1897, and in 1902 he bought Bateman's, a house built in 1630, which was his home from until his death in 1936. Kim was published in 1902, after which he collected material for Just So Stories for Little Children, published a year later. Both he and Josephine developed pneumonia while visiting the United States, from which she later died.

This decade proved his most successful, being awarded the Nobel Prize for Literature in 1907, the prize citation reading "in consideration of the power of observation, originality of imagination, virility of ideas and remarkable talent for narration which characterise the creations of this world-famous author". He was the first English-language recipient. At the award ceremony in Switzerland, Carl David af Wirsén praised Kipling and the English literary tradition:

> The Swedish Academy, in awarding the Nobel Prize in Literature this year to Rudyard Kipling, desires to pay a tribute to the literature of England, so rich in manifold glories, and to the greatest genius in the realm of narrative that that country has produced in our times.

Following this achievement, Kipling published Rewards and Fairies, which contained If, voted Britain's favourite poem in a BBC opinion poll in 1995. He turned down several recommendations for knighthood and was considered for Poet Laureate, though this position was never offered to him.

The sense of perseverance, honour and stoicism in If prevailed in many of his opinions, including that on the First World War. Writing in The New Army in Training in 1915, he scorned those who refused conscription, considering

....what will be the position in years to come of the young man who has deliberately elected to outcaste himself from this all-embracing brotherhood? What of his family, and, above all, what of his descendants, when the books have been closed and the last balance struck of sacrifice and sorrow in every hamlet, village, parish, suburb, city, shire, district, province, and Dominion throughout the Empire?

This attitude saw him encourage his son, John, to go to war, and he was promptly killed at the Battle of Loos in September 1915, aged 18. Last seen during the battle stumbling blindly through the mud, screaming in agony after an exploding shell had ripped his face apart, Kipling would write—

"If any question why we died
Tell them, because our fathers lied"

—perhaps betraying the guilt he felt at encouraging his son to go to war and finding him a position in the Irish Guards through his friendship with commander-in-chief Lord Roberts, for whom he had established The Friend in Bloemfontein. His death inspired much of Kipling's successive writing, notably My Boy Jack and a two-volume history of the Irish Guards, considered one of the finest examples of regimental history. Ironically, though his writing and his political position had arguably cost John his life, after the war he became friends with a French soldier whose copy of Kim, kept in his breast pocket, had stopped a bullet and saved his life. For a while the book and the soldier's Croix de Guerre were with Kipling, presented as tokens of gratitude, and they remained in contact, though when Kipling learned of the soldier's child he insisted on returning both book and medal.

He kept writing until 1930, though at a considerably slower pace, and to less success. His death, already once incorrectly announced early by a magazine in a premature obituary (and to which he responded "I've just read that I am dead. Don't forget to delete me from your list of subscribers") came on 18th January 1936, at the age of 70, from a perforated duodenal ulcer. His coffin was carried by, among others, his cousin the Prime Minister Stanley Baldwin, and his marble casket covered by a Union flag. He was cremated at Golders Green Crematorium in Northwest London and his ashes are buried at Poets' Corner in Westminster Abbey, alongside the graves of both Charles Dickens and Thomas Hardy.

In conjunction with various earthly memorials which commemorate him, alongside his extensive writing, he has a crater on Mercury named after him. The question of memorial and monument is much-addressed in English Literature and, as various great authors and poets have agreed before Kipling's time, his memory lives on more vivaciously set in his words, far longer and better represented than it could set in stone.

Rudyard Kipling - A Concise Bibliography

Books
The City of Dreadful Night (1885, short story)
Plain Tales from the Hills (1888)
Soldiers Three (1888)
The Story of the Gadsbys (1888)
In Black and White (1888)
Under the Deodars (1888)

The Phantom 'Rickshaw and other Eerie Tales (1888)
Wee Willie Winkie and Other Child Stories (1888)
Life's Handicap (1891)
The Light that Failed (1891) (novel)
American Notes (1891) (non-fiction)
The Naulahka: A Story of West and East (1892) (with Wolcott Balestie)
Many Inventions (1893)
The Jungle Book (1894)
Mowgli's Brothers (short story)
Kaa's Hunting (short story)
Tiger! Tiger! (short story)
The White Seal (short story)
Rikki-Tikki-Tavi (short story)
Toomai of the Elephants (short story)
Her Majesty's Servants (originally titled Servants of the Queen) (short story)
The Second Jungle Book (1895)
How Fear Came (short story)
The Miracle of Purun Bhagat (short story)
Letting in the Jungle (short story)
The Undertakers (short story)
The King's Ankus (short story)
Quiquern (short story)
Red Dog" (short story)
The Spring Running (short story)
Captains Courageous (1896) (novel)
The Day's Work (1898)
A Fleet in Being (1898)
Stalky & Co. (1899)
From Sea to Sea and Other Sketches, Letters of Travel (1899) (non-fiction)
Kim (1901) (novel)
Just So Stories for Little Children (1902)
Traffics and Discoveries (1904) (24 collected short stories)
With the Night Mail (1905) A Story of 2000 A.D
Puck of Pook's Hill (1906)
The Brushwood Boy (1907)
Actions and Reactions (1909)
A Song of the English (1909) (with W. Heath Robinson illustrator)
Rewards and Fairies (1910)
A History of England (1911) (non-fiction with Charles Robert Leslie Fletcher)
Songs from Books (1912)
As Easy as A.B.C. (1912) (Science-fiction short story)
The Fringes of the Fleet (1915) (non-fiction)
Sea Warfare (1916) (non-fiction)
A Diversity of Creatures (1917)
Land and Sea Tales for Scouts and Guides (1923)
The Irish Guards in the Great War (1923) (non-fiction)
Debits and Credits (1926)
A Book of Words (1928) (non-fiction)

Thy Servant a Dog (1930)
Limits and Renewals (1932)
Tales of India: the Windermere Series (1935)
Something of Myself (1937) (autobiography)
The Elephant's Child (fiction)

Autobiographies and Speeches
A Book of Words (1928)
Something of Myself (1937)

Short Story Collections
Quartette (1885) – with his father, mother, and sister
Plain Tales from the Hills (1888)
Soldiers Three, The Story of the Gadsbys, In Black and White (1888)
The Phantom 'Rickshaw and other Eerie Tales (1888)
Under the Deodars (1888)
Wee Willie Winkie and Other Child Stories (1888)
Life's Handicap (1891)
Many Inventions (1893)
The Jungle Book (1894)
The Second Jungle Book (1895)
The Day's Work (1898)
Life's Handicap (1899)
Stalky & Co. (1899)
Just So Stories (1902)
Traffics and Discoveries (1904)
Puck of Pook's Hill (1906)
Actions and Reactions (1909)
Abaft the Funnel (1909)
Rewards and Fairies (1910)
The Eyes of Asia (1917)
A Diversity of Creatures (1917)
Land and Sea Tales for Scouts and Guides (1923)
Debits and Credits (1926)
Thy Servant a Dog (1930)
Limits and Renewals (1932)

Military Collections
A Fleet in Being (1898)
France at War (1915)
The New Army in Training (1915)
Sea Warfare (1916)
The War in the Mountains (1917)
The Graves of the Fallen (1919)
The Irish Guards in the Great War (1923)

Poetry Collections
Schoolboy Lyrics (1881)
Echoes (1884) – with his sister, Alice ('Trix')
Departmental Ditties (1886)
Barrack-Room Ballads (1890)
The Seven Seas (1896)
An Almanac of Twelve Sports (1898, with illustrations by William Nicholson)
The Five Nations (1903)
Collected Verse (1907)
Songs from Books (1912)
The Years Between (1919)
Rudyard Kipling's Verse: Definitive Edition (1940)
The Muse Among the Motors (poetry)

Travel Writing
From Sea to Sea – Letters of Travel: 1887–1889 (1899)
Letters of Travel: 1892–1913 (1920)
Souvenirs of France (1933)
Brazilian Sketches: 1927 (1940)

Collected Works
The Outward Bound Edition (1897–1937, 36 volumes)
The Edition de Luxe (1897–1937, 38 volumes)
The Bombay Edition (1913–38, 31 volumes)
The Sussex Edition (1937–39, 35 volumes)
The Burwash Edition (1941, 28 volumes)

Poems
Departmental Ditties and Other Verses (1886)
Barrack Room Ballads (1889, republished with additions at later times)
The Seven Seas and Further Barrack-Room Ballads (In various editions 1891–96)
The Five Nations (with some new and some reprinted and revised poems, 1903)
Twenty-two original 'Historical Poems' (1911)
Songs from Books (1912)
The Years Between (1919)

Posthumous Collections
Rudyard Kipling's Verse: Definitive edition
A Choice of Kipling's Verse, edited by T.S. Eliot

In addition Kipling wrote and published many hundreds of poems too numerous to include here.